RISE

Little
DOZEN
press

Rise

Published by Little Dozen Press
Stevensville, Ontario, Canada
www.littledozen.com

Cover design by Mercy Hope
Copyright 2015

ISBN: 978-1-927658-33-8

BOOK 5 OF THE ONENESS CYCLE

by Rachel Starr Thomson

Little Dozen Press

2015

VIA DEL SOL, AD 1392

All morning the dream lay heavily on Teresa's mind, with her through all of the terrible tasks that were quickly becoming mundane. It was the stench that finally pulled her out of her reverie and fully back into the real world. As much as they burned incense and filled the air with perfume, there was no negating the stink of the disease.

It was the smell of death encroaching.

Teresa could not help but wonder if it was the smell of her own death and those of her sisters in the abbey. Perhaps it was. But they recognized in the plague the work of darkness, of chaos, and as Oneness, they knew their duty to stand against it. They had begun by going out and ministering to the sick in their own homes; then, as more and more families began to abandon their sick, they brought them to the abbey to care for them there. Almost overnight, the limestone edifice was transformed into a hospice, as the people of the outlying towns and villages brought their dying on carts and stretchers and left them to the care of the Oneness.

With her thick, dark hair knotted behind her and her sleeves rolled up to her elbows, Teresa sat beside one of the innumerable beds on the floor and wiped the brow of a dying girl with a wet cloth.

The girl was young—only perhaps sixteen summers. But any beauty or youth in her appearance had been ravished away by the plague. She burned with fever now, her eyes bright but unseeing, her skin white as parchment.

Teresa spoke to her of the Oneness as she tried to make her more comfortable, but what passed into the girl's mind she did not know. The stench in the hall was such that Teresa fought to keep herself open, focused, and calm. She wanted to run. But could not allow herself to do so.

The morning had passed when she felt a hand on her shoulder and looked up to see the bent form of Mother Isabel standing behind her.

"It is time for you to go back to your room now," Mother said, "and paint for us."

"Paint? But Mother . . . thirty new ones came just last night. Surely the Spirit cannot mean for me to . . ."

"Others can nurse. Only you can paint. There is a deep purpose in your gift, child. I sense it."

"But surely it would be selfish to leave the dying and pursue my own ends."

"Surely, if they were your own ends. But they are not. They are the Spirit's ends. No gift is given for the bearer alone. It is given that it may be given again. A seed grows a plant that bears more seed. If the seed refused to sprout, how would we eat the harvest?"

The hand on her shoulder lifted. "Go now. I will sit with this one."

Teresa looked down again at the girl. "I fear she is not long with us. I would bring her into the Oneness, but she cannot understand me."

"That too is in the Spirit's dominion. Do not take on yourself responsibilities you cannot fulfill. Go and fulfill the ones you can."

Teresa whispered a prayer of thanks to the Spirit as she passed out of the hall and into the east wing of the abbey, where the sisters had their chambers. The smell was not so bad here. The corridor was open to the outdoors, arches allowing in the warm breeze of the countryside and with it scents other than death. Flowering trees. Warm earth. The sky was brilliant blue, faintly streaked with white cloud. A canopy touched by a Master Painter.

Not one person in the abbey could have moved Teresa away from the sick beds or prevailed on her to paint at a time like this, except for Mother Isabel. Teresa was bound to her by a vow of obedience and so had no choice in the matter. A good thing, she admitted to herself, because although she could not sense the purpose that Mother swore to, there was some wisdom in her words. Death could not be allowed to cause all good things to cease. If one of those good things was her paintings, then she would paint in defiance of chaos and in celebration of life.

Her quarters were at the very end of the wing, expansive

compared to those of all the other sisters. Prepared wood panels and easels, gifts from a local woodworker, leaned haphazardly against one wall. Wide windows opened to the gently rolling hills, terraced to the south with vineyards, wooded to the north, and fading into blue before her. In the winter they would cover the windows with skins to keep out the cold, but for now, her room was open to the sky. A pale road looped up and over the hills to the east, leading to one of the larger towns. For the moment the road was devoid of travellers.

The sight, so peaceful, took her breath away. Yes, she had seen it a thousand times before. But now its goodness revealed itself to her anew. She had not known what to paint today, but she decided in an instant that these hills, this sky, that road would be her subject.

She wanted others to see their beauty with open eyes.

She wanted the dying, especially, to see it.

Carmela, a dear sister, had convinced her yesterday to allow her to take some of her best work and set it up in the hall where the dying could see them. Teresa had found the thought mortifying and forbidden it at first, but Carmela was so sure it would do them good. Teresa acquiesced at last.

And last evening, as she passed through the hall with a bucket of water and a dipper to cool their feverish tongues, she had seen some of the more coherent among the victims lying on their cots and basking in the sight of the paintings. Even smiling.

So Carmela had been right, and Teresa would bear whatever mortification came with the idea that her work should be displayed and treated as . . . well, as anything at all.

That memory was a strength now as she laid out brushes and

Rachel Starr Thomson

jars of pigment and went to mixing her paints while she gazed at the blank panel before her. Strength to focus, when other voices in her head were telling her she ought to be with the sick.

Sometime in the first twenty minutes her attention fixed itself on the panel, and then, lulled by the even rhythm of putting of a preliminary wash of colour over it, she thought again of the dream.

Her hand stopped, the motion of painting stilled.

She came back to herself suddenly, and jumped to realize someone was standing in the doorway.

"I'm sorry to startle you," Sister Carmela said.

Carmela was one of the younger sisters at the abbey, three years Teresa's junior. Long, thick golden hair, braided and looped behind her head, framed a childlike face with large blue eyes and a straight nose. She looked like an aristocrat, which in fact she was—but like the others, she had cut ties with the family of her birth when she became One.

They had not, however, entirely cut ties with her.

"Did you need something?" Teresa asked, hoping her tone wasn't terse.

"He is coming again," Carmela said. "I wish he wouldn't."

"Here? Now?" Teresa wrinkled her nose. "It defies reason. Most people run from death."

"We don't," Carmela pointed out.

"But he is not one of us."

"Assuredly he is not. Teresa, I do not wish to see him. Would you . . ."

"Deal with him for you?" She sighed. "Very well."

The young man in question was a choice of Carmela's parents. Handsome, foreign, and both wealthy and titled, it was no secret that he was their best hope for enticing her to leave the life she had chosen and return to privilege. Likewise, it was no secret that Carmela had no interest. But he kept coming—why, no one was sure. The sisters tolerated his presence and hoped he was coming because the Spirit was drawing him into the Oneness. Teresa had taken to managing his presence for Carmela, showing him around the abbey, conversing with him, and occasionally attempting to put him to work.

The Oneness in general didn't care much about money, titles, or looks, and the sisters of the abbey at Via del Sol were no exception to the rule. Especially not now, with so many lives in the balance and more work to be done than the sisters could do on their own.

"His note said he would arrive within the hour. About now."

Teresa removed her apron and laid down her brushes. "You might have warned me earlier."

"You were busy."

"Aren't we all," Teresa said quietly. She smiled at her friend. "I'm sorry. I am glad to help you."

Carmela smiled back, relief showing in her wide blue eyes. "You're a good friend, Teresa. I don't want him to think he might succeed in his object . . . or for my parents to think it. I hate that they send him here even with all that is happening in the countryside."

"Perhaps they want to draw you away from this place of death," Teresa said. "They do love you, though they do not understand your choices."

Carmela bit her lip. "Yes. In a way, that makes it harder. If they had simply disowned me, I think I could grieve and move beyond it. But their wanting me back is a hard burden to bear."

Teresa wiped her hands with a rag and hugged her friend around the shoulders. "The Spirit's plan has not yet come to fruition. Perhaps even this will have a role to play."

* * * * *

She spotted him as she approached the door to the garden where he often waited. He was early. Not a tall man, he was nevertheless commanding. With a firm jaw and close-cut blond hair—northern features—he was broad-shouldered and aristocratic.

"Good afternoon, Franz," she said as she stepped into the garden. Thick-trunked olive trees drooped long branches over the wall surrounding it, shading the purple flowers that grew in abundance around a moss-covered well. He leaned against the stones of the well, his quick eyes lighting up when he saw her.

But her attention was drawn away from him to the boy standing with him. Small, thin, with a shaggy mop of dirty, dark hair, and eyes too intelligent for his age—and the first signs of fever burning within them.

In her dream he had been much older, but she recognized him immediately.

Rise   11

And with him, the unmistakable mark of the Spirit's plan. They were meant to meet this day. They were meant to meet, and to become something to one another that would grow into the dream haunting and inspiring her every thought.

She reached out silently, seeking to know if the boy was already Oneness. He was not.

She knew that would quickly change.

Perhaps this was why Franz had so stubbornly continued to come to the abbey—because he was intended to bring this boy here, though he himself was probably unaware of that. Sometimes people chose to act in concert with the Spirit. More often the Spirit simply seemed to direct their steps, turning the paths they walked in whatever way the Invisible decreed.

She would have gone to address the boy directly, but Franz seemed to sense her intent, and he moved to position himself between them and reached for her hand, bowing as he kissed it.

"You look well today," he said.

The words felt particularly inane in this setting, with the child behind him clearly ill.

"As do you," she responded, "but this boy is not. I see fever in his eyes, unless I miss my guess."

"Indeed," Franz answered, "and so I have brought him to you. His parents were afraid to keep him at home, and I felt your sisters could do him some good."

Yes, Teresa answered in her heart. Far more than you know.

Of the sick who came to them, adults and children alike, most were dying. But some would survive.

This one, assuredly, would survive.

"How did you come into his company?" she asked.

Franz moved aside at last, allowing her a clear look at the child. The boy was perhaps ten. He looked at Teresa with the same intensity she knew she was bestowing upon him. The gentle green of the garden framed his skinny, tattered form.

"His parents recognized me as a frequent visitor to the abbey and accosted me on the village street as I passed by. They were bringing him here themselves, but decided to entrust the last of the journey to me."

Inwardly, Teresa winced. Many were afraid of the abbey— of the death congregating there. But surely this child felt the abandonment, having been left in the care of a stranger to be entrusted to the care of more strangers.

"Did they give you their names? Any instructions?"

"None."

Chances were, then, that they did not expect—or want—the child back.

She fought back a deep sigh, not wanting the boy to hear it, and instead extended her hand and a smile to him.

"Well," she said. "Tell us your name."

"Why does it matter?" the boy asked. He did not take her hand. "I am going to die anyway."

"I assure you," Teresa said, "you are not."

Franz made a sound, but she ignored him.

"How can you say that?" the boy asked. "Hundreds of children die in your house. It is the place where people send death. That is what they say."

"Many have died," Teresa said, "and many more will, for the disease is terrible and we know no way to defeat it. But not everyone will die. And you will certainly not. For you, this will be a house of life. I promise you that."

The more sensible side of her said that she ought not to make promises, that she might be interpreting her dream all wrong.

But she had long ago learned that the sensible side of her knew very little of the Spirit's ways and deserved very little of her trust.

Franz was listening intently, far more so than the boy. The boy was simply staring at her, as though his ears struggled to take in her words, and then, before she could react, his eyes rolled back and he fainted. She was just quick enough to catch him, and to be shocked—despite all of the illness she had seen in the last few weeks—at how little he weighed.

Franz maneuvered quickly and deftly behind her, taking the boy from her tenuous catch and lifting him up in his arms. "Show me where to take him," he said.

She led him through the door and down the arched corridors to the great hall where the sick were laid out, side by side, the sisters caring for them, the air thick and choking with incense and the unmitigated stink. Almost as soon as they entered the room, she heard herself saying, "No . . . no, this is not the place. Come with me."

She turned, noting the way Franz's hungry eyes swept the room and took in every detail, and led him out of the room and down the corridor to her own quarters. She opened the door to a mess of pigment jars and wood panels and light and air flooding in through the windows. Once again, she turned to see Franz's eyes quickened, drinking in every detail. It was not right to have a man in her quarters, but what could she do?

She pushed a mass of painting equipment off her bed and motioned for him to lay the child down. "Here."

"These are your quarters?" he asked.

"Yes."

"Your paintings?" He straightened from laying the child down and turned to take in the panel she was working on, as well as others leaning against the walls.

"Yes, they are mine." She wished he would leave so she could tend to the child without his intrusive presence, but she chided herself—the Spirit had brought Franz too. There must be some purpose in it. Some way she could minister to his soul, though his body was healthy.

"Yours is a remarkable gift," Franz said, bending close to one of the paintings. "I have some knowledge of these things. With some training, you might go all the way to the royal courts."

She flushed. "My gift is not for kings, Franz Bertoller. It is for the sick, and for the Spirit."

"Does the Spirit care nothing for kings?" he asked, a hint of teasing in his eyes. "Is that why you and your sisters insist on treating me like a commoner?"

"The Spirit is not a respecter of persons." She did not apologize for his taking offence, real or affected.

"Nevertheless, I could provide you with training."

"Thank you," she said, "but I do not wish it. My life is here, as are my duties."

The emphasis on here once more directed her attention to the fact that this man was standing in her private quarters, and they were alone but for an unconscious child who could be of little assistance even were he awake.

Not only were the circumstances improper, but for the first time in Franz Bertoller's presence, Teresa felt a threat in his manner—he was always intense, always drinking in his surroundings, but now that intensity, that drinking in, was trained on her.

It was a deeply uncomfortable feeling.

"My apologies," she said, "but I must ask you to leave."

"I see," he answered. "Of course. Tell me, where can I find your sister Carmela?"

It was a deliberate provocation, and she knew it. She could hardly require him to leave the grounds entirely, but nor could she leave him to wander without a hostess, and if she abandoned her post, she would be leaving Carmela to a situation she had promised to help her out of.

"A moment, then," she said. "Just let me tend to the child, and then I will attend you."

He nodded and moved to a corner of the room, both giving her space—for which she was grateful—and gaining a better vantage point from which to watch her. She tried not to think about the second factor as she made the child comfortable and coaxed him back to consciousness. From the looks of him, lack of food and sleep had contributed as much to his faint as the fever, which was low.

Throwing propriety to the wind, she called out to Franz.

Rachel Starr Thomson

"Please, go to the kitchen and find porridge and a spoon. I want to feed him."

Amusement settled on his face, but he did not protest, and she gave him directions to the kitchen. While the nobleman was gone, Teresa spoke quietly to the boy, who gazed at her with a solemn expression. How much he was taking in, she did not know, but he settled back into the bed, squirming a little as he did.

"You are safe here," she told him. "Safe and wanted. My sisters and I will care for you until you are well. And you too will become one of us."

He frowned at that and managed to say, "I cannot become a sister."

She laughed. "No, but you can become Oneness. And you shall. I know, because I have dreamed of it. What is your name?"

"I am Niccolo," he told her.

"And when did last you eat, Niccolo?" she asked.

"I don't know. It has been days."

"Days."

"My parents said I was going to die anyway."

"They were wrong." She kept her voice steady, not betraying her anger at a mother and father who would stop feeding their own child. Yet, she knew the poverty of some in the countryside was desperate. Perhaps there were other children to feed. Perhaps they felt they had no choice.

She smiled at Niccolo as she reached out and smoothed a long, sweat-thick lock of hair from his brow. Her soul was bonding to this child, her heart mothering him even as her hands followed her natural impulses. She hoped he would come into the Oneness very soon.

Franz reappeared, not carrying the called-for porridge himself, but ushering it in via the helpful hands of one of the older sisters. He looked much like a master ordering a servant, which bothered Teresa a little, but she was too grateful for the food—and the sister's company—to dwell on that overmuch. The sister sat on a low stool across from the bed and watched while Teresa helped the boy sit up and hold his bowl and spoon. He seemed capable of feeding himself. The sister fidgeted, and Teresa felt her impatience to be going. There were needs. Great needs. Every hand ought to be engaged in meeting them, not in chaperoning. But Franz did not seem inclined to leave the room.

The boy took his first few bites tentatively but gained speed as his strength began to return, until Teresa had to put out her hand to slow him down lest he make himself sick. She supervised his eating until the last drop of porridge was gone and then helped him lie down again—he seemed exhausted by the surge of effort. His face had gone white and his hands shook.

"Sleep," Teresa said, making up her mind to leave him alone—though her heart wanted to stay. "I'll come back to check on you. Just sleep for now."

He nodded, but his eyes were already closing of their own accord, and when she looked back just before stepping out of her quarters, she was sure he was asleep.

April's newest sketchbooks were full of fires.

Trees, forests, graveyards in flames. Cities in flames. People in flames. But nothing burning—everything simply wreathed in fire, filled with it, purified by it.

The pictures would likely disturb anyone else, so she didn't show them. She wasn't sure why she drew them—because, she thought, she was searching her own memory for a clear picture of what she had seen. She wanted to see it again. Clearly. In a way she could grasp.

She had been through the fire. Had been filled and purged by it. But she could hardly describe it, even to herself. It was the greatest mystery of her life.

Nick, she knew, had been stealing her journals and sketchbooks and looking through them with rapt attention, completely without her permission. He always returned them, and she let him be.

He Joined one day while pouring through her fire sketches.

She felt it the moment it happened—the coming of one boy's soul into the Oneness. The affinity that had always been there between them, the empathy and tacit understanding of one another's lives, gave way to something much deeper, closer, and more raw. She was perched on the roof when it happened, looking out over the bay, wearing a toque and wrapped in a warm blanket. It was November, the ocean air was damply cold, and fog lay out over the water. The boy's Joining came as warmth and a layer of strength in her bones.

"It's about time," she said aloud.

She sat on her bed now, going through her own pictures—all of them except those in the book Nick had most recently filched. Searching. Wind shook her window with a blast.

She couldn't find what she was looking for.

Looking at the pictures was like gazing at a veil drawn across a reality that looked something like it—as though someone had painted a landscape on a curtain and then drawn that curtain across the real thing.

"Where are you?" April asked, speaking out loud, as her fingers and her eyes searched the lines of fire. "Why are you so hard to see?"

Because I am in you, came an answer. You can't see what is behind your eyes.

She paused. "Is that also why you're so hard to hear?"

Because I sound like your own thoughts? Yes.

She smiled. "I can hear you now, at least."

But there was no answer to that.

Everything had changed for April, first in the water, then in the fire. In ways she was hard-pressed to explain, although she had tried to tell Richard—the wisest and most mature among them. But even he did not seem to understand that she had encountered—something—outside of what Oneness usually knew. That the Spirit had spoken to her, and had filled her, and burned her without burning her, in ways she had never experienced or heard of anyone else experiencing. And because of it, her entire understanding of the Oneness was changing. Of the Oneness, of the world, of herself.

Changing, and yet she couldn't articulate the change. Couldn't figure out what it all meant, didn't even know how to differentiate between the old and the new. And yet the dividing line was clear. Her world was not the same.

She was not the same.

Her door cracked and Nick's head popped in, only to be withdrawn almost as fast. But she had caught his eye.

"A-ha," she said loudly. "Caught red-handed. Get in here."

He obeyed, sheepishly entering with a sketchbook in his hands. She cleared a pile of other books and loose papers from the bed and gestured to the open spot.

"Sit."

He did, laying the sketchbook with the others.

"Why are you taking my drawings?" she asked.

"To learn," he said carefully. Like a schoolchild giving the right answer, even though he knew it was not the true answer.

"To learn what?"

This time the answer was even more tenuous. "How to draw?"

"I know you're only looking at the fire pictures."

"How do you know?"

"I spy on you. 'Fess up."

He grinned, not meeting her eyes but tracing a line on the bed with his fingers. "I wanna learn about what happened to you."

"You could just ask, you know."

"I didn't think you wanted to talk about it."

"It isn't easy to talk about." She frowned. "But I'm willing to try. Not overly many people seem to want to listen."

That was probably crossing the line, she decided; she shouldn't really be confessing her frustrations to an eleven-year-old, especially not one brand-new to the Oneness.

"Well," she said, trying instead to revisit her memories and put them into words, "you know how you felt when you Joined the Oneness?"

He nodded but didn't say anything. So she carried on, trying to describe his experience the way she remembered it from her own childhood conversion. "Everything changes. One day you're just yourself, and the next minute you've become a part of something that covers the whole world. You can feel the hearts of other people and they're all beating along with yours, and you can feel their happiness and their hurts and their hope. And it all becomes part of you, and it makes you feel strong. Becoming One is the most amazing feeling in the world."

He nodded. She'd gotten it.

"So," she continued, "what happened in the fire . . . it was like that. But different." She looked down at the books and flipped open the broad cover of one. The first drawing was not fire, but water—water and a deep, brooding darkness in the centre of it.

"It wasn't just the fire," she said. "I encountered the Spirit before that in the sea. In a dark place where it was . . . creating. Birthing something."

She looked up at Nick and could see that he was lost. And impatient to get on to the fire part. So much for her sympathetic audience.

"In the fire," she said, "it wasn't . . . it wasn't a fire like we burn downstairs when it's cold. The flames were real, but not physical. Well, they were physical. But . . ."

She stopped. Nick was watching her expectantly, and clearly unimpressed at what he had so far.

"It's hard to explain," she said.

"Why did the people die?" Nick said. "And you didn't?"

She just stared at him.

Leave it to a child to ask it so bluntly.

That was the question, wasn't it?

Franz Bertoller, their old enemy, had died. His henchmen had died. Jacob—one of their own—had died.

But she hadn't. She'd walked off the pyre burning from the inside out, and the flames had been like air and like blood and like life surging through her. She had ushered the girl, Miranda, out of the flames. And Reese had not died. Reese had seen David vulnerable, about to be consumed like Jacob was consumed, and she had covered him with her body and saved him.

So they three had walked away, and left everyone else in ashes.

The police had filed their report as a freak fire, suspected to have been fueled by gasoline simply because of its intensity, that had killed a number of visitors who were paying their respects at a local cemetery. In the middle of the night. Obviously there was far more to the story than that, but other than testifying to the presence of whatever people they could identify—including Jacob, who was a murder suspect and wanted back in custody—the Oneness hadn't talked much. They had just insisted they were all at the cemetery to pay respects to a mutual acquaintance. Lieutenant Jackson, who miracle of miracles remained friendly—if frustrated—to them, grumbled and complained at their inadequate explanations, but he confided to Reese that he was glad to see Jacob gone and just as glad to have her out of the picture. The whole story was full of holes, but no one—as yet—had a better one. Lieutenant Jackson was in charge of the case and seemed inclined to let it lie.

"So?" Nick pressed. "Why did they die?"

"I think . . . because they couldn't be in the Spirit's presence."

"Aren't we all in the Spirit's presence? All the time? Richard says the Spirit is like the air we breathe."

"It's true," April said. "But this was different. Kind of like if you tried to drink a concentrate before you diluted it."

"Huh?"

"You like orange juice?" she asked.

"Yes. Mary gives it to me whenever I want it."

"Well, have you ever tried drinking it before she mixes it with water?"

"Yeah," Nick said, looking slightly guilty. "One time I got a can out of the freezer and ate it with a spoon."

"And it was a lot stronger than the juice, right?"

"Yeah."

"It was like that. Like normally we're in the Spirit's presence, but it's diluted. And that night it wasn't; it was so strong it burned up anything that wasn't really part of it."

Nick wrinkled his nose. "I think it's kinda dumb to compare the Spirit to orange juice."

She punched him. "Fine. Go bother somebody else."

"So how come Jacob died? He was one of us, right?"

"I don't know the answer to that," she said. "I wish I did. I've thought about it a lot. Tried to ask Richard. But it's just one of those things we don't understand."

Nick flipped open another sketchbook and stared intently at the drawing in the centre. It was one of the most personal, one where she'd come closest to really capturing what had happened. The drawing showed a person wreathed in flames, and the fire was forming another human shape around it. It was impossible to tell whether the flames came from the human figure or whether the human figure was created by the flames.

"This is so cool," Nick said. "I can't believe this happened to you and you can't even talk about it."

"Hey. I tried."

He made a small noise that might have been a snort.

She sympathized.

"My mom is coming over," he announced suddenly.

"Oh. When?"

Shelley had lived with the cell for a few weeks before going back to her house and Nick's dad—who, they had learned, was an on-again off-again part of her life. She'd agreed to let Nick stay with them, which seemed best for everyone. Now that he was Oneness, April couldn't imagine him ever leaving. There didn't seem to be too much threat of that; Shelley hadn't come for a visit for the first month after she left. Nick acted like he didn't care, even that he was glad she stayed away, and April knew exactly what mix of emotions and opinions he was actually carrying around with him. Her mother had never once come for her after she became One. Before that, in the whirlwind few years that were foster care, interaction with her mother was forced and miserable. Her father's total absence was court-ordered and for everyone's safety. Becoming One gave April a place of safety and warmth and love, security she had never felt with her parents or in the system, and yet sometimes at night she cried because she wanted them.

Against every shred of reason.

"Today," Nick said, trying to sound casual. "She called last night and told Mary she misses me."

April just looked at him, and let him look at her, and neither of them said a word. They let the connection between them do all the talking. She understood. That was all she could really offer him.

Nick popped his head up a minute later. "Hear that?" he asked, a goofy grin lighting his face.

She had—a summons, deeper than words. Richard was calling the cell together. It was one of those things you couldn't feel before becoming One, and Nick obviously loved the sensation.

They met downstairs in the common room. Mary and Diane were already there, putting tea on for everyone with the help of eleven-year-old Alicia, and Melissa was sitting in her usual place on the couch, propped up on cushions and surrounded by books. Reese, Tyler, and Chris came in a few minutes later, ushered in through the outside door by a gust of snowy wind. Richard stood by the fireplace, leaning on the brick mantel and surveying the little group as they came together. His face was serious but not grim—an observation that made April aware that a sinking feeling had gathered in her stomach as soon as she heard the summons. She worked to let go of it now. The battle had been so fierce for the last few months, it was hard to believe they were being called together for something un-terrible now.

On the mantel over the fire hung the picture she had painted while Melissa played the piano—the bay in summer, and over it, the light that was the Spirit. She let her eyes linger on it, trying to probe that light. The light that hid in dark places under the sea and broke forth as fire in the midst of its enemies . . .

Richard let his eyes rest on each member of his cell as they entered and took their seats, holding steaming mugs of tea and chattering lightly to each other. April tore her gaze from the painting and met Richard's, and she smiled. For years the cell had been only herself, Richard, and Mary. The family had grown. But the original three would always be special to each other.

Richard cleared his throat as Mary finished serving and took her seat beside Melissa, resting a motherly hand on Melissa's feet, curled up under an afghan.

"You're all very good at this," Richard said with a smile. "Everybody's here . . . nobody lagging on answering that summons."

"We wouldn't dare," Chris said, and the others chuckled. He didn't have to say why—that they'd grown hypertuned to anything that might signal danger. But everyone had seen the lack of tension in Richard's face, and like April, they had relaxed into this meeting. They were Oneness, and they battled alongside each other. This afternoon they would just be together. And hear what Richard had to say.

"Well?" Mary asked, smiling. "Why have you called us together?"

"One simple reason," Richard said.

And then, to April's surprise, he turned to her.

"April has something to say," he said. "And we need to help her say it."

April looked out at the expectant faces ringing the room where she was most at home and found herself completely at a loss for words.

"I do?" she said.

"You do," Richard said confidently. "You've been living a story out that means something to all of us. I just thought you should share it."

"You did."

"Yes," Richard said, smiling, "I did."

April had been standing, but she dropped into an empty chair. "Richard, I don't have words. I've been looking for them. Trying to figure out how to say it . . ."

"I know," Richard said. "So don't talk. Use paint."

"What?"

"You heard me." He gestured to the far end of the room, where an easel and canvas stood waiting. They'd had it there since the day April painted the bay and the Spirit; she hadn't used it. "You know something happens when you paint. Stories start telling themselves. So tell us this one."

"Why?" she asked, her throat going dry.

"Because we all need it," Richard said. With everyone watching, the cell leader squatted down in front of April and took her hands. His brown eyes met hers. "April, you tried to tell me what had happened to you, and I did a bad job of listening. But I need to know what you saw and heard. I need to know what happened to you. We all need to know it. These things weren't just for you."

April nodded slowly, and went to the canvas with an almost wooden step. She picked up a paintbrush and started trying to visualize what she would paint—

And then abruptly laid it down and turned. "I can't. No. I'm sorry, Richard. I can't do it."

He frowned—his expression still compassionate, but concerned. "April, I know it must be hard. But we are One."

She shook her head. "But this isn't for all of us. What happened. I mean, it is . . . but I can't give it to anyone else. I shouldn't. It's too sacred for that."

"April . . ." A warning tone had entered his voice. She saw disapproval—and on Mary's face too, and some of the others. "I don't understand," Richard said. "To hold back what the Spirit has shown you—to keep it from the Oneness—that's selfishness, April."

She might have crumbled under that, but for the stubborn determination rising in her. And frustration at his inability to understand.

Reese spoke, surprising them all. "I understand."

"What?" Mary asked.

"I understand," Reese repeated. "She isn't being selfish. Listen, I walked on the edge of exile for a while. Almost followed in the footsteps of those who cut themselves off, like David and Jacob did. And I wouldn't trade the Oneness for anything. But I learned something in that fire too—and through the whole journey. Some things are not all about the group. Some things are just about you."

"That doesn't make sense," Mary blurted, but her expression seemed more troubled than the discussion warranted. "David would have said that."

"Actually," Reese said quietly, "David said the opposite. When I was sure the Spirit was leading me, he said I was a troublemaker. But I wasn't wrong. Those who trusted me were right to trust me. David tried to use our ways against me."

April listened and felt, as Reese spoke, a threat.

She went cold.

The threat was coming from Richard.

Hands shaking, she stuffed them in her sweater and moved

away from the easel. "I'm sorry," she said. "I can't show you what happened to me. Maybe there's a reason I can't really even talk about it. Maybe it's meant to be kept secret."

A knock at the door—loud and abrasive—rescued April from having to say more. "That's Shelley," she said. "We have to break up this meeting anyway." Her eyes pleaded. "Richard, something's going on here that I don't understand. You're scaring me. And I can't talk about this."

His eyes clouded, and she knew she'd hurt him.

"I'm sorry," she said.

"Let's answer the door," was his only response.

Julie should have been the last person Andrew Hunter expected to see when he arrived home from work, but she was not. True, she had not communicated with him in fifteen years; true, she had told him back then that they were through forever unless he was willing to join the cult as she had; and true, the police had officially pronounced her dead. Eyewitnesses said she had been shot. But Andrew knew that no body had ever been found, and he knew the other eyewitness report—the one that hadn't made official record.

That Julie had been shot, and killed, but also that she had been raised to life again. By a light. By something totally inexplicable.

Thanks to Chris Sawyer, Andrew had gotten his daughter, Miranda, back. He'd been doing his best to father and get to know her, assuring her that her mother was all right without promising her too much. But he was sure Julie would show up.

And when she did, he wasn't surprised.

She was waiting on his front porch as he pulled up after work. He'd picked up Miranda from school and dropped her and a friend off at the friend's house, so he was alone.

He was glad for that.

He recognized Julie immediately, despite the years that had passed. Her face was a little more lined, her figure a little fuller, but in essentials she hadn't changed a bit. She was sitting on his porch swing—one he'd been meaning to put away for the winter—with her hands clasped in her lap, just waiting. Her blue eyes alighted on his car the moment he pulled up, but she didn't move. Just waited for him to approach.

He spoke first. "Hello, Julie."

"Hello, Andrew." She bit her lip. "I guess this is a surprise."

"Not really," he said. "Miranda's with me. I thought you'd be along."

Her forehead wrinkled. "You didn't think I was dead?"

"I had good information that said otherwise."

"Maybe we need to talk about a few things."

"Maybe we do."

He unlocked the front door and pushed it open. "Please. After you."

She got up and entered the house gracefully, heading for the living room as though she knew exactly where to go. He sat, but she did not—just stood beside a free-standing lamp as though she was going to turn it off.

She turned. "First off, I can't tell you how sorry I am."

He cleared his throat and tried to hold his voice steady.

"For what, exactly?"

"For everything, Andrew."

He cleared his throat again. "Considering how things ended between us, I think we should try to communicate as clearly as possible. Make sure nothing's getting lost in translation. Don't you?"

"Okay." She breathed out, rubbing her hands together. She wore a wool sweater and a long, multicolored skirt, and she looked young and as beautiful as ever. His throat was throbbing. He waited.

"I'm sorry for the decisions I made. I'm sorry that I didn't trust you. I'm sorry that I believed Jacob over you and that I let his fearmongering affect my mind and my heart so strongly. I'm sorry that I decided a fear-ruled life was best for me and for our daughter, and I'm sorry that I acted out of fear toward you. I'm sorry that I saw you, and treated you, as the enemy. I'm sorry for shutting down early on, and for all the half-answers and the half-truths, and I'm sorry for everything I led you to think—and for the way I left. I'm sorry for that more than anything. I never should have gone. I never should have abandoned you. I never should have believed the community was more important than you were. That Jacob and his teachings mattered more than our family."

Her eyes were glistening with tears when she finished and looked right at him, waiting for a reply.

He wasn't sure what to say. "Wow. You've really thought things through."

"I've had a lot of time to think."

"I tried to reach you for fifteen years."

"I know."

"I never remarried. I never even divorced you."

"I know." Tears slipped from her eyes in the lamplight. "And I'm grateful."

"Do you want to come back?" Andrew asked. "Are you grateful because I kept a life you could come back to?"

"Is that why you did it?"

"Yes. I gave up faith in you a million times. Told myself it was a lost cause. Told myself I should move on—that I was practically morally responsible to move on. But I couldn't shut the door. I couldn't close off the possibility of you coming home. Which means you have one more thing to apologize for."

But his tone broke on that last line—broke because he let it. So she could hear the emotion he felt and understand that this time, he wasn't really asking for a confession.

"What is that?" she asked.

"Tell me you're sorry for dying," he said, "and shattering all of my hopes, even though it was only for a little while. That news broadcast slammed the door I'd been holding open for a decade and a half."

"I'm sorry for dying," she whispered. "But not too sorry. You've heard of life from death?"

"It's a concept that gets touted. Mostly in speeches."

"Well, it's real. I did die, Andrew. I really died. I was shot. The news wasn't wrong."

"And yet here you are."

"And you knew I was still alive—you said so. How?"

"A little bird told me. Someone saw you . . . raised to life."

"And you believed them?"

"I saw some crazy things. Made believing in resurrection not so hard to do." He stood and held out his hand. "Besides, when you've been holding a door open for fifteen years, it's not so easy to accept that it's been closed on you."

Julie took his hand. Her skin, the slender fingers, the warmth . . . it all felt so familiar.

Like something from another lifetime.

They stood there in the lamplight, holding hands, and then he dropped hers.

"We can't just go back, can we?"

"A lot of life has happened in the meantime."

"But you're here because . . ."

"I want to start over. And because of Miranda."

He almost winced. "If it wasn't for Miranda . . ."

"Andrew, look at me." He did. Her eyes, so blue, were deeper than before—more alive, more sincere. This was not the woman who had lied to him and then abandoned him. Not the woman who had succumbed to deception and then deceived him in turn.

"I would have come back anyway," she said. "Just for you. Just to find out about that door."

"I don't really know why I held it open."

"Because you're a good man, Andrew Hunter. I don't really deserve you."

He couldn't argue with that.

But his heart was starting to believe she had come back.

And that made him happy.

* * * * *

Richard cornered April while she was back in her room, going over the journals again. "Can I buy you dinner?" he asked. "Fish and chips?"

"That's Nick's favourite," she said. "Yeah. Sure."

She hated the way her hands shook as they walked side by side through the cold evening air toward the pub down on the wharf. Hated the way she felt herself shrinking from the tall black man at her side, like he was—someone else.

Like he was her father.

Like she was desperately hoping the conversation tonight would go well so that she wouldn't have to face the consequences of someone else's angry mood and uninhibited tendency to react in rage.

But that wasn't Richard. That had never been Richard.

Telling herself that, over and over, didn't stop her hands from shaking.

They were seated in a rustic booth in the corner of the pub, under dim lighting, and the waiter brought them drinks while they took off their gloves and hats and settled into the warmth without talking. April's eyes stayed on the table surface, polished wood, until Richard cleared his throat and she dared look up at him.

His brown eyes were kind.

"I felt all that fear on the way here, you know," he said. "No use in pretending your hands are just shaking because you're cold."

"I'm sorry." She stuffed her hands in her lap. "I don't know what's wrong with me."

"I do. I asked you to invade your most private experiences and bring them out publicly for all of us, and I didn't check with you first. It was wrong. I'm sorry. If you felt threatened, that's my fault."

Her eyes filled with tears. "Richard, I know you wouldn't hurt me. I feel like a kid again, and I thought . . . I thought I was past all that."

"Sometimes wounds are layered. You don't have to apologize if something I did peeled back a layer and exposed more hurt."

"Thank you." She took a deep breath and tried to settle herself. "It's not just that, though. I don't know why I can't tell you what happened. I love the Oneness. I've spent most of my life sharing everything. So why do I feel like I would lose something if I tried to put what happened into words?"

Richard frowned, deep in thought. "Maybe . . . maybe because we're thinking about it wrong."

"Come again?"

"You told us what happened. Bertoller pushed things too far, you asked the Spirit to come, and a fire broke out and devoured everything except you and Reese, and David because Reese was shielding him. A fire that was the Spirit."

"Yes," said April. "But that doesn't really begin to describe it. You know that; that's why you keep asking and Nick steals my sketchbooks."

Richard chuckled. "He does, huh? I'll have to talk to him about that."

"Ask him about stealing orange juice cans out of the freezer, too. And eating them."

"Will do. In your sketchbooks . . . you've been sketching the fire?"

"Yes. Trying to see it again."

Richard nodded. April felt the last of her tension release, and she was in the presence, not of a threat, but of an old friend— one she loved and trusted. For an instant, it was like becoming One all over again.

"So," Richard continued, "you told us what happened, and yet we all feel like a piece is missing, and you can't express it. I think I might know why. Tell me something, April. The fire that started in that cemetery—did it go out?"

April started to say "Of course it did," but the words died on her tongue.

"No," she said. "No, it didn't. It's still burning."

"Inside you."

"Yes."

The word came out as a whisper.

"That's why you can't talk about it," Richard said. "Because of one of two things might happen: it might get out of control again, or you might extinguish it."

He was right.

"How do you know that?" she asked. "You're right—but why do you know what's going on inside me better than I do?"

"I think that's giving me too much credit. I just figured out how to put it into words. I can feel some of what you're feeling, you know." He winced. "I'll never forget the look on your face this afternoon."

"I'm sorry, Richard. You didn't deserve it."

"I did, though. And I needed it. It was a warning. I'm going to do my best to pay attention."

"What's going on, Richard? With me? Can you tell me that?"

She searched his face in the dim light, more grateful than she could say for his presence and his friendship and his wisdom. Even if he couldn't really help her now.

"You're a great saint," he said. "The Spirit showed me that when we lost you the first time. There's something in your paintings, and just in you—you're important, April. I think the fire has something to do with that."

"But I don't understand. I'm just me."

A memory came to her: the woman from the cloud who had visited her in the cave, who had been starved to death by the enemy six hundred years earlier because she too was a great saint. Teresa. She had said, "Not one of us knows who we are."

"And I don't like it," she went on. "Everybody wants to be somebody. But being somebody, and not knowing who? And being totally out of control? Not fun."

Rise   **41**

"Maybe the problem is that we are all somebody, and we need to know who we are, but we're not really prepared to handle that information."

She smiled. "That doesn't help at all."

"You're welcome."

"And what about you? You and your voice of authority. All that craziness you did during the battle. I think that all makes you a great saint too."

"Maybe," Richard confessed. "I don't really know."

"I wonder if we ever get to find out. Now that the battle's over."

He lifted an eyebrow. "What do you mean by that?"

"The fight changed all of us. Now we're back at peace. Does that mean we just go on living our quiet little lives and never finding out any more of what's really in us?"

"I doubt it," Richard said, pointing at her. "Because the fire is still burning in you. And fires have a way of growing."

She shifted on the hard wooden bench. "That is not a comfortable thought, Richard."

"Sorry, but I didn't say it to make you comfortable."

She sat back, letting memory play, while Richard gave their order to a waiter she was too distracted to really see or hear. "You don't think it would just break out again?" she asked abruptly.

"The fire?"

"Yes."

He asked the question slowly. "You don't have to answer this

. . . keep anything secret that you need to. But in the cemetery: did it begin in you?"

"Yes," she said, forcing her voice to be stronger than a whisper and not shake. It seemed important to be brave about this, bold.

She wasn't sure she'd realized it up until this moment, but yes. The fire had started burning in her, and then out through her, and then all of the destruction had come.

Richard's eyes were troubled. "Then if it's still burning, it might break out again. Yes."

"It killed people, Richard."

"Arguably only people whose time had come to die."

Her breathing was starting to come faster. "That doesn't make me feel better." She stood suddenly. "I think I need air."

He let her go, and she stood outside the pub, listening to the creak of the docks and the beat of waves, looking up at the moon in the cold air. She could see her breath, but it felt good—good to be out here, good to be cooling off. Her breath was still coming too fast, but the longer she stood there, gazing out at the moonlit water and the tall trees of masts clustered in the harbour, the calmer she felt.

What was it? The fire?

You know, a voice said.

But she ignored it.

Out here, in the cold, she had no choice but to ignore it.

The food would be getting cold, and Richard was probably polite enough to wait for her, so she talked herself into going back inside and rejoining him.

She felt all right now.

Everything was under control.

* * * * *

Andrew took Julie along to pick up Miranda. He didn't think seeing her would come as a shock; Miranda had been told early on that her mother was alive and had accepted that as true without question.

Julie got out of the car first, advancing tentatively and then breaking into a run to embrace her daughter, who raced down the sidewalk from the house to her. Miranda's school friend stood in the door, waving, and then gave up on getting Miranda's attention back and went inside.

Andrew's mouth was dry as he watched his wife and daughter embrace. The wife he'd lost. The daughter he had never known. It was impossible to quantify this moment, even to himself. Life from the dead, Julie had called it. That was what it was.

"But what kind of life?" he asked himself, muttering the words out loud.

He remembered the fire in the cemetery.

And the story of Julie's resurrection, which she had not yet fully told him.

And Chris's stories about the Oneness.

And about Jacob, and demons.

This would not be his old life back. Not for a moment.

"They're worth it," he said, again speaking out loud, like doing so would make the words more true. Or more convincing. He fixed his eyes on them, blonde head bent over blonde head, Miranda's arms around her mother's waist, Julie's shoulders bent as though she wanted to envelop her child entirely.

They were worth it.

Miranda pulled her mother the rest of the way to Andrew, her eyes shining. Those eyes melted his heart and strengthened his resolve. Yes, she was worth it. Even if the day came when their lives normalized so much that she turned into a normal teenager and didn't look at him with so much adoration. Even if someday she decided that she hated having a father. Even if he was bad at this. Which he very well might be.

He'd never had a chance to find out.

She was worth it. And he would do his best.

Julie's eyes were shining too, but not for him. She was happy, her eyes were glistening with tears, because of their daughter, with whom she had an actual relationship.

Suddenly the loss of the last fifteen years felt totally disorienting.

"And you are here, and Daddy is here, and we never have to be apart again!" Miranda was gushing, in that way she had that made her sound four years old. "We won't be, will we? We will never be separated again. Never ever."

Andrew reached out, resting his hand on her shoulder in a way that didn't yet feel natural. "If I can help it," he said, "that's how it will be."

Rise   **45**

He met Julie's eyes when he said it, and she nodded, but he saw the trouble there and knew this wasn't agreement. It was more like a truce. Because something was still unsettled between them, and while that thing remained, promises could not be made.

That thing was resurrection.

Julie's resurrection.

And the change—to everything in the universe—that it represented.

Niccolo did little in his first week at the abbey other than sleep and eat. He ate heartily and well, and every time seemed to collapse from the effort. He remained in Teresa's room—she slept on the floor—to which Franz Bertoller was not again admitted, though he continued to visit the abbey almost daily and asked faithfully after the boy. His earnest enquiries softened Teresa's heart toward him somewhat. He did not have to take an interest in the child, who had been thrust upon him by parents too negligent or too hopeless to love him properly. It spoke well of the nobleman that he continued to care.

Teresa spent her days alternating between her quarters and the great hall, where the sick and dying continued to come, to be sick and to die. Niccolo showed no sign of healing, but she had not forgotten the dream, and he was to her a symbol of hope—for himself and for the others. They would defeat this evil of disease. They would outlast it, and from its ashes would rise great good. She spent her nights sleeping fitfully and then rising to pray, spending hours on her knees at the boy's bedside.

Assurance that she would win the battle was no reason not to fight it.

Late one night, while she was on her knees, riding the river that was prayer, a painting came to her.

It had never happened like that before—that she simply saw the finished painting before she had even begun it. And it was not like anything she had painted before. It was colour, but without shape; a winding, twisting ribbon of light. Like water infused with fire.

And though she had never tried to paint in the dark, and had never interrupted prayer to do it, this night she felt sure that the picture in her mind was prayer. That she had no choice but to paint it. So she rose, as quietly as she could, and lit a candle— watching the boy intently to make sure he did not stir. He did not; his sleep was frighteningly like the sleep of the dead. But then, she reminded herself, could not many ten-year-old boys sleep like the dead? In the candlelight she prepared the panel and the paints, mixing pigment with water and egg yolk, and went to work. In time that she couldn't track it was finished.

Mother Isabel came in the morning, without announcing herself. Teresa looked up from sleep to see her standing there scrutinizing the work of art that was still drying before the window.

"I think," she said in her old, cracked voice, aware through who-knew-what clue that Teresa was awake and listening, "that in the royal courts they would tell you that you cannot just paint colours moving like that, you must paint things." She was silent a moment while Teresa waited in a state of unusual suspense. She had not known Mother's opinion would matter so much.

"But I think," Mother announced, "that they would be crackpots and fools, as usual. I don't know what you have painted, my dear, but it is beautiful, and I am glad to see that you are pursuing your vocation, even in the dark."

"I must confess, Mother, that I interrupted prayer to paint it."

"Nonsense. You prayed in painting it. Anyone can see that."

"That is what I thought. But I didn't know anyone else would agree."

"I agree. That will have to be enough. Now, how is the patient?"

Teresa cast a glance across the room to the boy, who, still pale, thin, and gaunt, was unmoved from sleep. "He sleeps and eats and I see no change."

"Still, the eating is a good sign."

"He will recover, Mother. I knew it when I took him in. The Spirit has shown me this. And more besides."

Perhaps the painting had made her bold. She did not know why else she spoke up about this now.

Mother seemed unfazed. "I would that the Spirit would show me more of his plan," she said. "This house of death is not the home I desired to make for the Oneness in the Way of the Sun. But Spirit willing, life will reign here again."

She turned from the painting and smiled at Teresa. "That is what I see in your midnight artwork. Life."

Teresa smiled back, tentatively at first but then broadly, accepting the praise and then basking in it. She was grinning like a child but could not bring herself to stop. She had not known it would feel so good to hear these words from someone she respected so deeply.

Perhaps she had not known how much a part of her these paintings really were.

"I think you should leave this one to sit here," said Mother, "where the boy can see it when he is awake. A feast for the eyes while he is feasting those threadbare bones. It will be healing to him. And to you too, I think."

"Am I need of healing, Mother?"

"If we are human, we are in need of healing."

She spoke the words in a way that carried deep conviction, and Teresa wondered something she had never wondered before—who Mother Isabel had been, before the abbey and before she had taken up mothering so many. Before she was Oneness.

Did that matter? Wasn't Oneness all of life, and everything before it to be discarded and counted as nothing, like Sister Carmela's wealthy family?

Until this morning she would have said yes.

But now . . .

"I am confused, Mother," she said.

"That is often a sign that the Spirit is speaking to you."

"But I thought the Spirit was not a source of confusion?"

"He is not. Our own hearts and minds are sources of confusion, and apt to be stirred up when the Spirit begins to speak truth. If we listen, the truth will clear up our mud puddles again. But it is not very comfortable or clear in the meantime."

The old woman turned to go. "The Spirit is working in you, Teresa. My advice is that you continue to let him. Paint in the dark. Entertain new thoughts. Above all things, do not try to control him. He is not to be controlled."

"He?" Teresa asked.

"Eh?"

"You called the Spirit 'he.'"

"Of course."

"But the Spirit is a force. A being that creates unity . . ."

"The Spirit is a person," Mother Isabel said, with more force than Teresa had ever heard her use before. "Do not let anyone tell you any differently."

The words spun in Teresa's mind. "But that is not how we speak of it . . . him."

"That is a tragedy," Mother Isabel said. "Do not let habitual foolishness blind you to the truth, when that truth begins to reveal himself to you."

And with that, she exited the room.

* * * * *

Miranda's childlike prattle did not stop the entire length of the drive home. For Andrew, the drive was surreal. As though the loss of fifteen years ago had never happened, and they were just an average suburban family on their way home. Except that the other children he had hoped for had never been born, his wife was a stranger, and his daughter—fifteen years old—sounded disconcertingly like she was four.

He chided himself for being annoyed. As Miranda started to talk about her friend from school, and the pretty way she decorated her room, and things the other kids had said that she didn't like, part of him wanted to tell her to grow up. He hated that response. This was his girl. His long-lost child. Shouldn't he just embrace her—embrace everything she was?

But something was wrong with what she was.

That conviction grew the longer the drive went on, until, when they reached home, he excused himself with a few words about needing to work on the truck and disappeared into the garage while Julie went to make dinner.

Just an average suburban father, he told himself, his head under the hood of his truck, a '79 Ford that he'd been meaning to help along for a while. Just an average father in full escape mode.

When Julie cleared her throat—loudly—from the door to the house, he didn't know how long she'd been standing there. He almost banged his head on the open hood.

"What are you doing?" she asked.

"Aren't you making dinner?"

"You're hiding. Why are you hiding?"

He turned and spread his greasy hands out, beseechingly. "Why are we fighting? We haven't even been back together a whole day."

She looked down, and he saw that her hands were wrung together. "I'm sorry."

"So am I." His voice softened, and he wiped his hands on

a rag and flicked the garage light off to go inside. But he didn't move. Julie just stood there, framed in the light of the house, and he stayed in the dark and avoided her gaze.

"What is it?" she asked again, but this time her voice wasn't demanding or accusing. She was asking sincerely.

He struggled for words. "Is Miranda . . . is she okay?"

Julie frowned. "She's been through a lot, but she seems fine."

"That's not exactly what I meant. It's . . . it's like she's not her age. Like she's years younger. Doesn't that bother you?"

"We wanted our children to take their time to grow up," Julie answered. He winced at that "we." We, the community. We, Jacob's followers. We, not Andrew, not the Hunter family.

"I guess I didn't expect much of her," Julie said, "or engage her as an adult . . . but all the children were like that. Innocent."

"Naive."

"You didn't want our children exposed to all the evils in the world either."

He sighed. "If it comes down to that, I still don't. There are a lot of evils in the world. But she has seen so much now. You said so yourself . . . she's been through so much. Why hasn't that . . . sobered her?"

"I don't know," Julie said slowly. "I thought . . . well, I guess I thought she just couldn't understand the gravity of it all. Because of her innocence."

"Do you honestly think that's a good thing?"

She thought over the question, and he was glad that she didn't react defensively. "I don't know," she said, finally.

Rise　　　　　　　　**53**

He reached for her hand, and almost to his surprise, she took it. It was the closest they had come, physically, in fifteen years—holding hands. Earlier in the living room and now here, in the meeting of the shadows of the garage and the light pouring out from the kitchen and the living room and the hallways and . . .

It struck Andrew suddenly, and hard, despite the way Julie's nearness was messing with him.

"Why are all the lights on?" he asked.

She let go of his hand and stepped back. "Are you worried about the electric bills?"

"No, I just want to know . . . who turned all the lights on? You didn't, did you?"

"No . . ." Julie turned and surveyed the house, flooded with light. Andrew was right. Every light within sight was on, not just the overhead lights in each room, but lamps too, and in the kitchen, someone had lit a row of candles on the counter.

"Oh," Julie said.

"I think," Andrew said slowly, "Miranda may not understand the gravity of everything that has happened, but it hasn't exactly all gone over her head."

"You're right. I'm sorry. I should have seen that more clearly."

"You were just relieved to be back with her," Andrew said. "It's okay. You're a good mother, Julie."

He spoke those words with conviction, even though he had never watched her parent. Had never even seen her and Miranda together except on the sidewalk outside the school friend's house, embracing, blonde head to blonde head. Even though he knew he disagreed with Julie's most fundamental parenting choice: to remove her daughter to a cultish community in the middle of nowhere. Even though he could see that something was wrong with Miranda's development, and Julie didn't seem to have really realized it until now, and even though it had taken his pointing it out for her to acknowledge that Miranda might be suffering a little bit of trauma.

He still believed it. So he said it again for good measure. "You're a good mother, Julie."

"You do not have any reason to say that," Julie said with the smallest of smiles. "But thank you. I'm glad you believe in me."

She turned to go inside, then hesitated and turned back. "And you're a good father. Anyone with two eyes could see that. Miranda adores you already." Her smile grew broader, and deeply genuine. "And I'm glad she does."

* * * * *

"Franz is so persistent," Carmela told Teresa as they drew water at the well in the abbey gardens one afternoon. "I have given up trying to drive him away; it is a lost cause." Her smile grew almost sly. "Besides, I think I have nothing to fear. It is you he wants to see, though you do not often appease him. I am more an annoyance than an object in his coming."

Teresa batted her friend. "Fie on you for implying that I should care whether he wishes to see me or not."

"He is handsome."

"And he is not One."

"No," Carmela said thoughtfully. "In truth, Teresa, I do not understand his coming here. He looks for glimpses of you, and evidences his satisfaction when you give him time, but he does not come for you only. He comes for the sick."

"To be of service to them? Then he is a rare noble."

"I wish I could say that were true," Carmela said. "He does help us in tending them. More and more lately."

"Then why do you doubt his intentions?" Teresa asked. She dipped into the bucket and used the water to wash her arms and face, its coolness a welcome balm. There was plenty of water after they made ablutions to take back for the sick. For these few moments of calm, she would enjoy the sun and the water and the quiet green shadows.

"I cannot say. Will you come and join us this afternoon? He is coming. Come and make the rounds with us."

"I don't want to encourage his intentions."

"Nor do I! But I have had little choice, and I think that your simply tending the sick alongside us cannot be seen as encouraging his suit. Will you do it?"

Carmela's eyes, large and blue as they were, always made her seem younger than she was, and the combined effect made it impossible to say no to her when she pleaded. Teresa chuckled and wondered how Franz Bertoller's attentions had managed to shift to her when someone as radiant and winsome as her friend was set before him—and all Carmela's family's wealth besides. But who could tell with men? Or with nobles.

"Very well," Teresa said. "Since you insist so insistently."

Carmela smiled broadly. "Thank you, dear friend. It would

ease my mind to know your thoughts—once you have observed his way with the sick, and with us."

But the event itself did nothing to ease Teresa's. Franz Bertoller came as always, dressed in workaday finery and oozing gentlemanly charm. He greeted them all and paid Teresa special attention, but he fell into the rounds with practiced ease, helping to carry water, to prop up those who needed to drink, and to light incense where the smell was especially bad. The sisters chafed hands and feet, emptied pans of waste, and sang and spoke to the suffering, even to some whose eyes showed no comprehension. Carmela closed the eyes of one who had died and slipped away to alert Mother Isabel. She would see to it that some of the stronger sisters carried the dead out. Franz's help might have been well appreciated there, but he did not offer it, and no one would ask.

But for all his surprising helpfulness, and the condescension he showed in working alongside them in the first place, Teresa soon saw what it was that made Carmela so uneasy—and so unwilling to say that Franz's reason for coming was to tend to the sick.

It was in his face. A rapt attention—an eagerness—to the details of disease and death. He showed no signs of sorrow or trouble at the wasting bodies and tormented souls on every side. Instead, he seemed to greet every new vision of the plague with unspoken enthusiasm. Like a student discovering new vistas in his chosen field of study.

But this field should not leave any human soul unmoved.

And Teresa realized something else.

There were four of them making the rounds together, along

with Franz, and as usual the sisters of the Oneness responded to their deep communion in impercetible ways as they worked. They knew when one needed a reprieve, when another's gifts would better suit the needs at hand, how to strengthen each other's hands and fill the gaps. They did not need to speak, as their hearts continued in communication deeper than words, and so they rarely did. But Franz's presence, Teresa realized as they moved from litter to litter, patient to patient in the hazy, stinking room, was like a boulder in the midst of their stream. He interfered with the flow, created friction, brought distraction—and more than distraction. In some way his being there fractured them.

Her paintings had been for some time now set up in the hall, positioned so that various of the sick could see them. There were more than one hundred of the diseased and dying lying on litters in the great room, and they so took Teresa's attention that she had ceased to notice or think about the paintings. But she happened to look up while she was talking to a dying man, a very old man who seemed to see in her his own daughter or perhaps a sweetheart from his youth, and saw Franz Bertoller examining one of her works with a look on his face that she could not describe.

It might have been anger or confusion.

And it felt like a knife to her heart.

* * * * *

"I need to speak with you about Franz Bertoller," she told Mother Isabel in the abbess's study that evening.

"The young nobleman who has been helping the girls?" Mother asked.

"The same."

"Speak on."

"I think we must tell him he is no longer welcome," Teresa said.

Mother Isabel frowned. "That sounds rather drastic. Do you have a reason for turning away help in a season when we need it so badly? I need not remind you that we number only thirty-two, and the plagued are more than three times our number. The young lord is not one of us, but his hands are not wasted."

"And yet, Mother, there is something deeply wrong about his spirit. Carmela told me of it—I thought as you do, but she urged me to come and see for myself. He does help us, but it is as though he rejoices in the plague."

Mother's frown grew deeper. "You would make him a monster. Those who are not One are not therefore our enemies, Teresa."

"I am bothered by his otherness," Teresa confessed; "it is a distraction as we work together, and I suspect he keeps us from drawing others into the Oneness while he is present. His being there scatters us. But that is not my primary objection. I tell you, there is something wrong in the way he looks at the dying. And the paintings."

The last three words escaped her mouth before she could recall them, and she immediately regretted them. Mother Isabel sat back and looked up at her, her eyes holding unmistakable reproof. "He criticizes your artwork, does he?"

"He seems not to know what to make of them."

"And that makes you wish that he would stay away?"

"Something about it troubles me deeply, yes. But it is not that alone, Mother; it is the other things I've said."

"I know it was not easy for you to bring your gift into the light," Mother said. "You are exposing your soul in your artwork. I understand that. It embarrasses you. And maybe you don't want this young man to see your soul, and maybe you are very troubled that when he does see it, he does not understand it. Even reacts negatively. Yes?"

That was all true, though Teresa hadn't understood it until now. She nodded, but let out a sigh of frustration. "It is true, Mother. And I am sure I need to be more humble, and to let the paintings serve others without wrapping myself up in them so much. I cannot deny that. But please, Mother, believe me. It is not for that reason that I am speaking to you of this."

"This young man," Mother Isabel said, in a tone that suggested she might not have heard anything Teresa had just said, "he shows some interest in you also, does he not? They say he has transferred his affections from Carmela, and her family will be very angry."

"That is true," Teresa said quietly. She cursed herself for mentioning the paintings—for turning the focus of this conversation inadvertently upon herself. It should have been someone else, she realized, to come to Mother Isabel with these concerns, someone who didn't seem so personally embroiled. Much as she hated to admit it, she looked like anything but an objective witness.

So she was not surprised when Mother said, "I cannot turn away help, Teresa. Not now. But I release you from any obligation to work alongside the young man. Keep your distance with my blessing, even should it mean that sometimes we are short-handed. But I wish him to continue lending his aid, and I hope that as he works alongside our sisters, his spirit will be drawn into the Oneness as all of ours have been."

Teresa nodded, gloom settling into her heart. This was not the conclusion she'd hoped for.

"Now, tell me, how is the boy?"

It took her a moment to understand the question. "Oh, Niccolo. He is doing somewhat better. When I go to check on him he is more often awake, and I think soon I shall have to find him a way to occupy himself."

Mother chuckled. "Yes, indeed. There is nothing more dangerous than an unoccupied child. But if he is doing so well, we shall soon have to move him from your quarters."

"He cannot be transferred into the sick hall," Teresa said, alarmed. "I think the air there is foul. I would fear for its effect on him."

"Mmmm, indeed. Another solution will have to be found."

"Yes." Teresa waited, but Mother seemed finished with the audience. She turned, hesitantly, to go, and blurted, "Mother, please, will you continue to think about what I . . ."

"Teresa, you are free from any need to consort with the man. That is all I can give you for now."

Nodding, she left the room unhappily.

Richard sat in the waiting room with his hands clasped between his knees, leaning forward. He hadn't bothered to remove his knit cap or gloves, despite the fact that the room was warm—overly warm, April thought.

Posters displaying various forms of disease in stages of bad to worse hung on the walls. Silent clusters of visitors sat together, mostly grim-faced; one woman chattered in Spanish to the man next to her. A much older woman in the corner of the room was silently weeping.

April felt overwhelmed by it all. By the people looking death in the face, and she could do nothing to help them.

She could not even help Richard, who looked grimmest of them all.

She had invited herself along, even though Mary was already going to accompany Melissa into the doctor's office, because she didn't want Richard to be alone. But for all her good intentions, he seemed pretty alone anyway.

It was so warm.

There was little question what the doctor would say. Melissa's last appointment had confirmed what they could all see in her face and the weight she was losing—that the miraculous halting of her cancer had ceased, and the disease was marching forward aggressively.

Richard still blamed himself for that. Even though they all, Melissa included, understood and had verbalized that there had been no other choice. It was that guilt, as much as the looming prospect of Melissa's death, that made his face so haggard and his shoulders so bent.

She wanted to say something. "It's going to be okay." Except it wasn't. "It's not your fault." Except it was. If Richard hadn't interfered with the children and challenged the hive, Melissa might still be facing a lifetime of music and fame and success.

She might still be facing a lifetime.

Richard was staring straight forward.

April stood suddenly and shed her coat. It was just so hot.

What is the point, she wanted to burst out, of being Oneness, of being a light against the darkness and holding the world together against the forces of chaos, if you can't even do a thing about death? If you can't stop one of your own from dying, if one of your own can actually die because she is faithful to Oneness, and if you can sit in a room full of frightened, dying people and do nothing at all to help or to stop it?

Richard looked up at her, his face suddenly questioning, and she realized she hadn't sat back down, and that her temperature was rising and she was fairly sure her face was going red and her breathing was getting short. Other people were staring at her now too.

"I'm sorry," she said. "I think I need to go outside for a minute. It's hot in here."

Richard had both eyebrows raised, his forehead wrinkled in question. At least she was distracting him from Melissa. She wanted to say something else, but her overheating body wouldn't allow for it. She turned and rushed out the door, dashed down the hallway, controlled her breathing as the elevator descended two floors, and ran through the revolving door into the cold air outside.

A grey drizzle greeted her, mixed with the sooty, exhaust-fumed air of Lincoln. Tall buildings on all sides marked out the downtown area where the clinic was located. She gulped in the air, grateful for it despite the pollution. Rain on the glass windows and lights reflecting off the water on the roads made everything seem darker and gloomier, and she shivered.

"So," she said out loud, not caring about passersby, "what good is it to be Oneness if you can't beat death? Answer that."

To her surprise, the Spirit did.

With one word.

Julie.

* * * * *

The first of Miranda's screaming fits struck the second night they were all together as a family in the house. Andrew came running and nearly bumped into Julie, who was running down the hallway from the bedroom at the opposite end of the hall—he had moved himself into the living room and given his own room to his wife, while their daughter occupied what had been a bare, optimistic spare room for years. A nightlight illuminated the hallway just enough to keep the two from colliding.

That seemed fitting. Andrew had bought that nightlight in a fatherly shopping fit fifteen years ago, assuming that his soon-to-be-born child would be scared of the dark. He had never thrown it away. And his child was scared of the dark. Or of something in it.

Despite every instinct screaming at him to burst through the bedroom door and slay whatever dragon was making his daughter cry, Andrew backed off and let Julie enter first. She went straight to Miranda's bedside, calling her name and snuggling onto the mattress next to her. Miranda woke up with an incoherent stream of words and then sobs, and she curled closer to her mother. Andrew opened the door wide enough that the glow from the nightlight could get in. He didn't want to flick on the overhead light and hurt anyone's eyes.

He wished he didn't feel so awkward.

"Hush," Julie was whispering. "Hush, it's okay. It's okay, Miranda. What's wrong, baby? Hush, hush."

Andrew stood in the doorway searching the shadows of the room for a dragon.

Or maybe for Jacob.

At this moment, he could kill Jacob. Probably it was best that the man was already dead.

Though that thought left him with an unsatisfied hollow in the center of his being.

Miranda was murmuring something, maybe telling Julie what was wrong, but Andrew couldn't hear from where he stood, and no one invited him in. He stood in the door for a few more minutes and then excused himself and stalked back to the living room, leaving the door open for the nightlight.

He paced in front of the couch in the dark. Cold illumination from a streetlight outside shone through a crack in the curtains. Andrew had never been an angry man, certainly not a violent one, but he raged now in the dim light. Raged silently and impotently.

Julie joined him and sat on the end of the couch an hour later. He had stopped pacing but could not lie down and rest, so he just stood there—a blank, restless knot of emotion.

Julie pulled her legs up and sat cross-legged, waiting for him to sit down too. He did, and took his glasses off the side table so he could make out her features as clearly as possible in the dark.

"Did you find out what was wrong?" he asked, surprised at how calm his own voice was.

"She had a nightmare. She wouldn't say exactly what."

"All that time and . . ."

"I can't make her tell me, Andrew."

"You were there an hour." He let out of a sigh of frustration and held up his hand to stifle any retort. "That's not what I meant. I'm sorry. This is not your fault."

"I feel helpless too," she said.

"I'm her father. I should have been there to protect her."

"You would have been. I took that choice away from you."

He peered at her through the dimness. Neither made a move to turn on a light. "You've gotten very honest since your death."

"I think resurrection leaves lies behind it. In the grave."

"Can you tell me what happened to you?" he asked.

She nodded and gazed over his shoulder, pulling up memories. "I thought I heard Miranda screaming outside. I rushed out of the house to help her—I thought she was across the street. I never found her. I did run into thugs, and they shot me. I didn't really have a moment to process any of it."

"It's what happened after that that I really want to know about," Andrew said.

"Are you sure about that?" Julie looked especially vulnerable in the dim light—but especially untouchable too, foreign and strange. As she was in reality. He thought over her question seriously before answering it, and found that a part of him—a large part of him—wanted to say no.

He didn't want to know what had happened. He wanted to know nothing at all about it. He didn't want to hear what Julie had seen or felt or experienced or why she was alive when she had been dead. All of that was so far out of his normal world, and so far out of his control, that he wanted it to stay out. Forever.

But he couldn't keep it out without keeping Julie out. And Miranda. Without closing the door he'd kept open for so long.

So he said, "Yes."

"I died," Julie said, very slowly. "But I didn't. Some kind

of separation happened. My . . . spirit, or whatever it is . . . separated from my body and didn't die along with it. But at the same time I knew the body was dying, and then dead; I could feel that happening. And . . ." She stopped. "Honestly, Andrew, I can't describe this part."

"Fair enough," he said.

"But then I could feel something breathing. It was this rhythm, inside me, coming through me . . . almost the way sound goes through you when the bass is turned up, but more than that, because I could feel it contracting and the breath rushing through me, and then suddenly my own lungs were breathing, and I could see light everywhere and feel warmth in every part of my body. My body, which was alive again, and I was back in it."

She stopped there. So he picked it up. "And then, according to witnesses, you disappeared. In a cloud of light."

"I don't actually know," she said. "I remember the light and the warmth, and the breathing. I can even remember feeling the alley underneath me, and the air—it was a hot night; the pavement was hot. And then I woke up. I don't know when I fell asleep or what happened in the meantime."

"You woke up. Not in the alley anymore?"

"No, I was in the woods. I thought I must not be in this world anymore."

"Like you'd gone to heaven."

"Yes."

"But you hadn't."

"No."

He could see it in her face—this was the part she didn't want to tell him, or didn't know how to tell him. This was the part that was going to change everything. He was tense. His hands and jaw were clenched. He tried to relax but he couldn't, didn't even really want to. He was waiting for a sucker punch and wanted to be ready for it.

"There was someone there with me, Andrew," Julie said.

"Someone. A person?"

"Not . . . exactly. But a personality, yes."

"And you talked and . . ."

"Maybe we should backtrack." She took a deep breath. "I'm Oneness, Andrew. Do you understand what that means?"

He couldn't keep the bitterness out of his voice. "Sure, Jacob talked about it all the time. Drawing apart to become the unified community of . . ."

"No, Jacob was wrong. He was promoting a mock-up of the Oneness, his own version. A mockery, really. Not the real thing. I never came into the Oneness while I was in the community, even though I thought I had."

"Okay." He blinked, a little confused but still resistant. "Okay, then, explain."

"You met Reese. And Chris, and Tyler, and some of the others."

"Yes. They helped me find Miranda."

"They really are Oneness. And Reese brought me into it . . . into them. The Oneness is . . . it's something supernatural. A real community, because when you enter it, you all become part of each other, and the spirit world opens up to you."

Andrew laughed this time, bitterly again. "You don't have to tell me about the supernatural. I saw the fire. And that freak trying to offer my daughter as a sacrifice."

It's no wonder, he told himself, that she's having nightmares.

"Sorry," he said. "So how do you get into this . . . Oneness?"

"It's hard to describe."

"No surprise there. Sorry again. Keep going."

"Reese visited me, and in her presence I could just feel the Oneness—like an open invitation. And I wanted it, so I accepted the invitation and it just happened. If it hadn't, I don't think I would have survived the shooting. I think it was being Oneness that saved me."

"Go on."

"The Oneness teach that the source of our unity is something called the Spirit. Some people call it God. It's the life force animating all life in the universe, breathing through everything, if you will—"

"The breath you felt bringing you back to life?"

"Yes." She nodded, and her face showed relief that he comprehended and that he was making an effort to understand.

"They also teach that while the Spirit is holding the universe together, and in a sense directing things and uniting things, there are other forces trying to tear it apart. Demons are a manifestation of that, but so are other things . . . disease, death. The most common words they use for that force are darkness and chaos."

"Common enough ideas in the world of men."

"True," Julie said, "but it's one thing to think things are a certain way. It's another thing to be filled by them. To be part of them."

She looked down at her hands, her face showing her struggle to put words to what she wanted to say.

"And it's another thing again if the Spirit, who is a part of me and is holding us all together, is not just some impersonal force, but is a person."

Andrew thought that over.

"Do you understand what I'm saying?" Julie asked. "When I became One, I knew something came into me—changed me—filled me. Something that was life and connectedness. I didn't know someone had come in. But that's what I know now."

"You're possessed," Andrew said bluntly.

"We are all meant to be."

They stared at each other.

"If you had to choose between me and . . . him? Is that the right word?"

"'Him' is better than 'it.'"

"If you had to choose between me and him, you would choose . . ."

"Him."

"And 'he' is different from Jacob because . . ."

"Don't do that, Andrew. Don't draw that comparison."

"I don't know why I shouldn't." He sat back, his head reeling. "You are telling me that I don't just have my wife back, I have my wife and some stranger who commands her loyalty more than I do, more than I can ever hope to, if I have to guess."

"It's not the same thing," Julie said. "It's different this time."

He stood and tried to keep his voice level, tried not to yell. "Why? Why is it different? How is it different? You're telling me that you're back, and you're willing to live with me, and our family is more important than anything, and you were wrong, and yet now you have some other Person in your life whose word is god. So promise me, Julie: promise me that this Spirit of yours will always put our family first and will never take you away again."

She just stared at him, dry-eyed—and he wished she would cry. He wished there were tears in her eyes to show conflict, to show that she didn't want him to yell at her, to show that she was wavering at all. But there were no tears. Just stoic courage and determination.

"No!" And this time he yelled. If he'd had something in his hands, he would have thrown it. "No, I can't do that again!"

He turned on his heel and stormed out the door, leaving Julie alone in the house with Miranda.

With Miranda, and . . . and the other Person living in her.

What was that even supposed to mean?

It was freezing outside. He stuffed his hands under his sweater and charged down the sidewalk, distractedly noting that a few cars were out, headlights sweeping the dark street—it was early morning, then, and people were on their way to work while his world fell apart.

All over again.

The day Mother Isabel cut off Franz Bertoller was the day Teresa walked into her quarters to check on Niccolo and found the nobleman there, staring intently at her patient—who was awake, and staring intently back.

When she walked in, instead of being startled, Franz turned and demanded, "Why is he healing? He ought to be dead. I saw the condition he was in when I brought him. What is giving him the strength to overcome?"

Taken aback, Teresa sorted through several possible answers and only voiced one: "What are you doing in here?"

He ignored her question. "Tell me why he is recovering."

"I don't know. But you, sir, are where you do not belong and are not welcome. Answer me: why are you here?"

Perhaps aware that she had some power in this situation that he did not, Bertoller toned himself down. "I was concerned for the boy's welfare. It has been some time since I was allowed to look in on him."

"You have not been allowed it now, unless you have gained some permission I am not privy to. But I very much doubt that."

"What are you afraid of?" he asked, and she saw the threat and desire in his eyes. "Does it bother you to know how easily I can access your quarters when I want to?"

"Get out," she said. "Monster. Get out."

"Why would you call me that?" He took a step closer. "What do you see in me?"

"I do not wish to talk to you."

"Do you want to know what I see in you?"

"Get out."

She cast her glance around the room, looking for something—anything—she could use as a weapon. To defend herself, if need be, or to chase him from the room if he refused to go.

"Don't be afraid," he said, his voice inexplicably soft, "I will go. And I do not want to harm you."

Those words shook her, because he meant them. And she glimpsed something in him as he spoke the words: an enormous capacity to harm, and to desire to harm, and a vulnerability toward her that made him unwilling to tap that capacity.

He left.

And she trembled—with anger, with a forceful lack of understanding, with not wanting to understand. Why was he vulnerable toward her? Why?

She went to Mother Isabel and relayed the whole encounter, and this time, Mother listened—perhaps because she could see how deeply troubled Teresa was. That this went far deeper than vanity. Teresa was responding to something in this man that was truly dangerous. Mother made no commitments, but Teresa knew she went to talk to some of the others immediately afterward, and within a few hours she found Teresa at work in the sick hall and made two announcements: that Niccolo was going to be moved out of Teresa's quarters and that Franz Bertoller was no longer welcome at the abbey. She would send a messenger and tell him so.

But the look on his face haunted Teresa, and the haunting grew the more she thought of it. Both sides of what she had seen: His ability, and desire, to cause harm—something she could only identify as evil. All human beings dabbled in corruption, but few seemed so wholeheartedly a part of it. And the other side, the vulnerability. The openness. To her.

A vulnerability that was something like love.

The haunting took the form of a question that shaped itself over days, especially after she knew the message had been dispatched and that, if he respected it, the nobleman would appear in the Way of the Sun no more: if a man so lost to evil was vulnerable to her, even in love with her, did she not have the responsibility to try to help him? To use this one open door to draw him back to the light?

Niccolo was a welcome distraction. The turn which had so fascinated Bertoller came fast and advanced even more quickly; he went from thin and wasting—despite the food he ate—to gaining weight, colour, and energy. In a matter of days he was awake more than he slept, and Mother Isabel was entirely right to move him from Teresa's quarters. He needed to be where others could keep a closer eye on him and where he could be given something to do. As his healing progressed, his personality began to show—a cautious solemnity, born perhaps of too much responsibility and too little care, gave way to curiosity and natural exuberance. Mother Isabel put him to work in the kitchen, but one too many spilled kettles and curious explorations into the pantry and the flour drawer ended with his exile by the exasperated older women who worked there. Deciding that his scrawny legs and skinny back were stronger than they looked, and that sun and air and exercise would only help his already remarkable recovery, Mother changed his responsibility to water boy. He hauled buckets from the well for hours, with plenty of being sidetracked in the gardens and courtyard and surrounding hills, but he tended to sidetrack only when the need was not urgent—so no one minded.

Teresa loved to see him entering the sick hall with water and scampering off again with the empty buckets. Though at first he tended to make his deliveries quickly, within a few days he was lingering at the side of the sisters who were tending the sick, and then taking up a dropper and offering water to some of the younger ones himself. Soon he was as familiar a face in the hall as any of the sisters.

Bertoller's absence was not marked or minded.

Only in the middle of the night, when she rose for prayer in the moonlight, did Teresa think of him. She prayed his name and thought on his face, and speculations as to how she might help him or what might have made him so soft toward her ran roughshod over her prayers. She sensed no answers, no guidance. But when she slept, more nights than not his face marked her dreams.

It occurred to her that she might, after the manner of women, be growing infatuated with the young nobleman. That

Rachel Starr Thomson

perhaps Carmela's family's scheme had found its object after all, if the target had gone slightly awry. But surely that could not be. Surely her heart was only yearning to save one who was deeply lost.

She wished she felt that she could trust herself. But who could truly know her own heart?

Perhaps some great saint in ages past could have delved the depths of her own motivation. Teresa could not, and the inability humbled and stymied her.

For multiple reasons, then, it was best that Bertoller was long gone. She wondered if he had left the country entirely and gone back to his own place of origin, somewhere in the north. Carmela's family would know, but they made no effort to come to the House of Death, as all the country was calling the abbey now. Rumours began to reach them that the people expected the plague to spread to the sisters themselves, and no one would survive. The Way of the Sun would become the Way of the Forgotten.

Clearly, the rumourmongers had not seen Niccolo running to and from the well, bounding over the low courtyard walls, chasing grasshoppers in the sun, appearing from the vineyards with a grin and a dirt-smudged face whenever he was wanted.

But Niccolo was an aberration. Even a freak. No matter how the others were tended, as the incense burned and the haze and fever choked the hall with heat, no matter how many ladles of water were given, bowls of porridge were fed, songs were sung and hands were held, the others continued to die.

At first, most of the patients to come to the abbey had been elderly. Now, as their bodies were moved to the graveyard, more and more of their spots were taken by children.

Teresa could not sleep. It was a hot night, and her thoughts were full and restless. She rose and took to the corridors, following her feet wherever they led.

They led her to the sick hall.

The hall was in deep shadow, though groans and rustling indicated that many of its inhabitants did not truly sleep. A few of the sisters tended patients in the farthest corners, but Mother had ordered that as often as possible, the sisters sleep at night. Though it meant some would die alone, even the Oneness could not go on forever tending the sick without taking some care for themselves.

Teresa walked the rows in the darkness, praying silently over the restless and the still. In the darkness, made murkier by the still-lingering haze of incense, she nearly walked right into another night roamer—one she had not seen in part because he was so small.

"Niccolo," she whispered. "What are you doing here?"

Large eyes gleamed up at her. "I do not want them to die," he said.

"Neither do I."

"Why did I heal, and they do not?"

"I cannot say. We all wish we knew that."

"The painting helped me," he said, in a tone of voice that said his words were conclusive. "Make more of them, and bring them out here. They will help people heal." He spoke in a whisper, as though he didn't want to wake anyone, but so loudly that his voice carried to the far corners of the room.

"There are already paintings out here," Teresa said. "You know that; you've seen them."

"Not those," Niccolo insisted. "More like the one you painted for me."

Teresa was going to tell him it wasn't exactly for him, but she refrained—perhaps, in the Spirit's wisdom, the painting had been for him.

There was no question that Niccolo's change for the better had happened shortly after she left it where he could see it.

Her hands tingled uncomfortably, even painfully. "Why are you up?" she asked.

"I want to help them."

A rebuke rose to her lips, but she didn't voice it. How could she? They all wanted to help. And Niccolo's desire was so pure, so urgent, that she could feel it like a pulse in the air.

And then there was the dream.

Maybe, against all appearances, there was something he could do.

She didn't expect that he would tell her what that something was, but he did.

"You will teach me to paint as you do," he said. "And you and I will both paint pictures that make the Spirit visible, and when the people see them, they will be healed."

"Is that what I did?" she whispered. "Did I make the Spirit visible?"

His bad attempt to stay quiet rasped harshly. "Of course."

"And you think we can do it again?"

But she knew the answer to that.

She'd seen the dream.

If anyone in the abbey had the latent power to bring healing amid the sights and stench surrounding her, it was Niccolo.

But surely before he could do such a thing, he must open his heart and be Joined to the Oneness.

She began to say so, but something in his eyes caught her off guard.

Here, in the dark, in the haze and the sickly smells, she could see his eyes as though they glowed. They were blue—intense blue, and shifting like smoke or like fire. Yes, like fire. In the blue she could see what looked like tendrils of flame, like the Spirit itself . . .

She shook her head to chase away the vision. She was not sure she could handle seeing what she was seeing, and she wondered if it was a mere illusion, brought on by exhaustion and hope and all the other things she was feeling.

His eyes were just a boy's eyes.

But she had seen it.

She was meant to ask him, "Are you One, Niccolo? Do you wish to become One?"

But she could not. The question was not right—it was out of joint, somehow, with what she had just seen. The boy was filled with the Spirit. With a flash of insight she realized that in trying to make Niccolo come into the Oneness as she understood it, she was about to do what Mother Isabel had warned her not to do—to try to control the Spirit.

He, Mother Isabel had called the Life Force that animated

and filled and inspired her. As though the Spirit were a man.

A wild and unpredictable man, no more to be controlled or leashed than the very wind.

Her throat tightened.

She would very much like to know such a man.

Niccolo was peering curiously at her.

"You should return to your bed," Teresa said. "It is late, Niccolo. Sleep."

"You also."

She cuffed him lightly. "Don't you know better than to command your elders?" But she smiled in the shadows, and she thought he saw it.

* * * * *

April fretted over what the Spirit had spoken to her outside the clinic all the way home, and continued to do so after they arrived and Melissa retreated to her room. Richard was too deeply engrossed in the medical news to ask April why she had run from the waiting room or why she seemed so agitated now, although under normal circumstances he would have noticed. Mary was likewise preoccupied.

The results of the latest testing had come in: things were bad, and the doctor wanted Melissa to start radiation in three days. He'd given her pills to start taking.

The march to death was fully underway.

One word: Julie.

Julie held the answer, somehow. The key.

The key . . . to something April was only beginning to grasp. An understanding, a full realization or manifestation. Of just what they were who called themselves Oneness; of just what the Spirit was, this being they breathed like air and took for granted as they did blood in their veins or clouds in the sky; of what their battle really—truly—meant.

And the key to what was still burning inside April with a power she was growing afraid of.

April went up to her favourite spot on the roof, not bothering to bundle up despite the wet chill in the air. The shingles were slick. She stayed up there only a few minutes before jumping off a low point and walking down the cobblestone street. Too much energy. Too many questions.

She had no idea how to find Julie. Chris claimed the woman had been resurrected after her murder at the hands of some of Clint's—Franz Bertoller's—goons. He'd been told by an eyewitness, a boy Chris said was some kind of watching angel. Apparently he had run into a lot of those.

Her feet picked up speed, and she broke into a run. It felt good to move, to fly through the cold, to throw herself into the pull of gravity and pelt downhill.

When the supernaturality of the Oneness had entered her life, she had gladly fled the foster system and a short lifetime of abuse and neglect into its warm arms. Then, supernatural had meant safety, fulfilment, true humanness, love. Everything she'd always known she wanted.

Not this.

This was out of control. Frightening. Violent.

Dangerous.

The pounding of her feet became the pounding of fists on a wall, on a door, the threat of a beating, the breaking of glass—

She pulled herself up short. She had reached the harbour. She was overheating. Hyperventilating. Terrified.

"Julie," she said out loud. "Julie, Julie, Julie. I have to find Julie. She can help me. That's what the Spirit said."

Saying it all like some kind of mantra helped as she hoped it would. The cold, low clouds began to drizzle, and she stood by the water and let the rain soak her. Her hair strung around her face and clung to her skin. She raised her arms and let the rain wash her down.

She talked to herself out loud. "There has to be some way to track Julie down. She has a daughter . . . Miranda. I remember. I walked her out of the fire, and Chris found her father. Julie will go to her. That's how I'll find her."

She knew she was talking herself as though to a patient in shock, or someone very old or very young who had to be coached through reality, who couldn't be trusted just to understand. It felt appropriate. She felt as though she were talking herself back from some kind of ledge.

Maybe because she had somehow split herself in two and one part of her was talking to the other part, it took her a moment to realize someone else was saying her name. She whirled around. Nick was standing on the street corner a few feet away, clutching an umbrella and wearing woolen gloves with his long-sleeved T-shirt and jeans.

"You should wear something warmer," she said.

He just wrinkled his nose at her, crossing the street.

"Okay, fair enough. Give me that." She took the umbrella he offered, clutching it like a lifeline.

She'd never been so glad to see anyone. Kind of embarrassing that she needed a kid to rescue her, but there it was. Apparently being alone was a terrible idea right now.

They started the trek back up to the house.

"What were you doing?"

"Just going out for a run."

"Didn't you know it was going to rain?"

Yes. No. Maybe. She hadn't stopped to think about it.

"Do you remember Miranda?" she asked.

"Yeah. She's weird."

"Weird how?"

"Immature."

April didn't bother hiding her smile—half-amusement, half-reproof.

"She is," Nick insisted.

"Any idea where she lives now?"

"She's not my girlfriend, okay?"

"I didn't say that. Don't be a goon. I just wondered if you knew where she lives. I know you went with Richard to visit her once or twice."

"They were staying in a safe house then," Nick said. "I'll bet

Chris knows, though, huh?"

He was probably right. Relief swept her at that—maybe finding Julie wasn't going to be insurmountable obstacle she'd almost imagined it being.

"Why do you want to know?"

April briefly considered the wisdom of confiding in a little boy. But this much couldn't hurt. "I want to talk to her mom."

"She got shot."

"And she didn't stay dead."

Nick grinned. "I know. It's cool. Like the fire."

"You're really eating all this stuff up."

"And you're scared of it. How come? The fire didn't kill you."

April wasn't sure she wanted to consider the question. "I'm not sure. Mind your own business."

"It's my business too. We're Oneness."

Touché. Still.

"That doesn't mean we share everything. Remember the meeting the other day?"

"I remember that when you first got outta the fire, you weren't scared of anything. And now you're scared of everything."

That actually hurt. All she could find to say was, "Hey."

"It's true," Nick said, sticking out his jaw in a peculiar way he had of showing stubbornness.

"How did the day with your mom go?"

"Okay, I guess. She bought me a soda."

April decided to let the rest of that lie. She very much wanted Shelley to be a good mother, and was painfully aware that she wasn't. But there was hope. Shelley might become One . . .

And end up a basket case like me?

She answered herself on that one: Hey.

Water was starting to collect in the gutters, and April stopped Nick from dragging his feet up them to make waves that would slosh over his feet. He was wearing sneakers, and they weren't exactly waterproof.

Nick brought up one more thing before they reached the house.

"Melissa's going to die, huh?"

April paused a half-step. "I think so. Yeah."

"And we can't even stop it?"

April thought of half a dozen wise things to say and decided none of them were worth saying.

"That's stupid," Nick announced.

"We can't do everything." She snapped the words, more than she meant to. "We fight how we can."

"It's not enough." He folded his arms, and out came the jaw again. "Well, it's true."

"You just have to accept some things, Nick. Death is one of them."

His voice followed her in the front door. "That's dumb."

Rachel Starr Thomson

Niccolo and Teresa took their plan to Mother Isabel in the morning, and she approved it so quickly that Teresa wondered if she had some other motive in doing so. There followed lessons: lessons in crushing pigments and mixing paints, in colour, in brushwork, in form, in shadow. Everything Teresa knew. The boy—peasant boy from some village Teresa did not even know the name of—learned it all in a matter of days, and from then on the work was pure joy. He layered paints over panels like a thing inspired, and though every time Teresa feared that his attacks of brush and colour would end in a formless mess, everything he painted came out looking like—

She did not know how to describe it.

Like life.

Like living.

Like love, joy, exuberance.

Like the Spirit itself.

"Himself," Mother Isabel corrected her when she confided her feelings about Niccolo's work.

"Why do you call the Spirit by that name?" she asked.

But Mother Isabel only smiled wisely and mysteriously and gave no answer.

"Teach him other things also, Teresa," Mother said on the third day of Niccolo's art lessons, while she surveyed the sketches and preliminary paintings he had done. "The Spirit has brought him to you. Teach him all you know. Teach him your compassion. Teach him how you care for the sick. Everything."

Teresa opened her mouth to ask about Niccolo's status in the Oneness, but once again the words died away on her tongue, and she simply said, "Yes, Mother. I will do as you say."

Niccolo tackled everything Teresa gave him to do with the same unbridled eagerness and a willingness to work and learn that she had never seen in anyone. Perhaps because of his willingness, he was also a quick study in nearly every endeavour, and Teresa found herself taxed in trying to find things for him to learn and to do.

But it was the paintings he loved most and believed in most deeply. When he had finished his first, it had not even dried before he was running with it to the sick hall, unable to wait to place it where the dying could see it.

It would seem arrogant except that he was so convinced that he had himself been healed by the effect of such a painting, and that he seemed to regard his ability to make the same sort of painting to be nothing other than a gift given him in answer to prayer: a way he had been given to save others.

And his faith did not seem misplaced. In the first week that his paintings began to grace the hall, along with more done by Teresa's hand—every one a surprise to her, though none as purely inspired as the one she had done during prayer in the middle of the night—one of the sick children began to recover. And then another.

There was indeed some strange grace in the pictures of the Spirit.

So it was that when things took a turn for the worse after all, and the deaths began to multiply, when the incense was not enough to keep out the flies and other vermin, nor to cover the encroaching scent of death itself, Niccolo was of all most devastated.

On a morning when eight were carried out, three of them children, Teresa found the boy sitting on the stone wall in the garden, arms clasped about his thin legs and head on his knees, weeping.

She held back a moment, unsure of whether to intrude, but her heart so moved toward him that she could not stay away. She sat beside him and touched his head, entwining her fingers in his hair.

"Weep on, my lad," she said. "There is good reason to break your heart. But a new day will come."

He looked over at her and pushed his head into her hand like a small cat would do, his face streaked with tears. "But why isn't it working? I was so certain it would work. That if they could only see, they would live."

"To see . . ." Teresa frowned as she began to understand how little she understood of this boy. "What is it you want them to see, Niccolo?"

"I want them to see what I see. He makes everything alive. Everything. So why is it not working?"

"It . . . it is, Niccolo. Remember the children who recovered? Some have gone home! We are not the House of Death anymore."

"But now everyone is dying."

"Not everyone," she said.

That very evening, as shadows began to fall across the terraced hills and valleys, as moonlight picked up the pale roads and caused them to shine, the first of the sisters began to fall ill.

For months now they had seemed under supernatural protection, and Mother Isabel had intimated she believed they were—that somehow Oneness were immune to the terrible plague. No more.

The kitchen ladies who had been driven so to distraction by Niccolo's antics were two of the first to fall ill, and Niccolo ran frantic water to them, and bowls of porridge that they were too sick to eat, and blankets for their feet, and when the first of them died, he buried his face in Teresa's skirts and howled with grief.

His painted panels presided over the hall of the dying as more and more of the sisters fell ill, and those who remained ceased sleeping or resting or caring for themselves as every moment was given to the sick. Niccolo served among them, brow constantly furrowed, a blur of motion that outpaced all of them.

In the early hours of one morning, Teresa sat beside Carmela, who burned with fever, chafing her hands and whispering to her. Carmela motioned toward a far corner of the hall, though she did not waste energy on trying to speak. Teresa looked up to see Niccolo wrestling a larger wooden panel off its easel.

She jumped up and went to him, stopping him just as he was trying to heft it up off the floor and onto his shoulder.

"Where are you going with that?"

"I am taking it away."

"Why?"

"Because it is useless."

"The Spirit gave it to you, Niccolo. Remember? You told me what these paintings are for—to place here so that the dying may look on them and be healed."

"It was a stupid, childish idea," he said.

And he sounded so much older than he had the day he told her his plan. So much older that it made her heart ache.

"It was not stupid," Teresa said. Gently, she pried his fingers from the painting and lifted the panel back onto its easel.

"And this is not yours. You painted it for the ill, and your gift came from the Spirit. So you have no right to remove this. Leave it be, Niccolo. Let the Spirit determine what sort of work it does."

He turned and ran from the room, but she had seen in his eyes, even in the darkness, that he knew she was right. He was running not in petulant anger, but to go away and think over what she had said and pray.

She had never seen a child so filled with the Spirit.

She returned slowly to Carmela while doubts tried to push their way into her own mind. Niccolo was right, after all. Their hopes for the paintings had not come to pass. The death toll grew higher and more costly to them as their own began to cross over, to become a part of the cloud. But she had to believe the unusual works of art had a purpose beyond what she could see. And that the power of death was not strong enough to overcome the plan of the Spirit who was life.

"Please," she heard herself whisper in prayer as she sat beside her friend, "be the stronger—be stronger than death."

She did not know what good it would do to beg someone to be something. If the Spirit was not stronger—if, after all, chaos was the superior force—asking that it might be different could do no good.

But prayer was all she could offer.

And so offer it she did.

* * * * *

"Do you know where they are?"

Chris didn't have to think about April's question. "Sure. Andrew left me his address. I think he thought we might need to reconnect at some point."

"You're right that Julie will go there," Reese said.

The pair sat together, Chris's arms wrapped around Reese's shoulders, she leaning back against him. Their usual posture these days. Appearances suggested that the broad-shouldered young fisherman was still worried that he would lose Reese again. No one blamed him.

They were an oddity—a romantic pair within the Oneness. But no one questioned that they were connected for a reason, that this expression of unity was beautiful and right. Chris had begun talking about marriage the day after Reese came home. They kept their plans mostly private, but April expected them both to turn up wearing wedding bands any day.

"Why do you want to find her?" Reese asked. "Not that I think it's a bad idea—I think it would be good for her to reconnect with us anyway."

"I have questions," April said simply. "I think Julie can help me with them. It's just a hunch . . . call it a Spirit thing, I guess."

Reese glanced up at Chris and then looked back at April. "Things really changed for you in that fire, didn't they?"

"Yes. But I'm not sure I can explain how."

"It saved my life," Reese said simply. "I was steps away from turning against the Oneness. From going beyond redemption."

"Is anyone ever beyond redemption?" Chris asked, clearly bothered by the statement. April noticed the way he tightened his arms around Reese.

"What changed your course?" April asked.

"The fire itself. It was like—like the Spirit was in it. In a more pure and powerful way than I had ever experienced before. Like it was the Spirit. And I wanted it. Him. More than anything. I couldn't turn away. It took me a while to realize that was it . . . at first I thought the fire just burned the bitterness away. But it was more than that. It gave me a desire stronger than revenge."

"And then you saved David," April said, marvelling.

"Yes." Reese looked sad. "I think because of Bertoller. He

was beyond redemption. David wasn't. I couldn't let David go that far too, not if I could do something to help him. He was a friend once. More than that, he's a man. A human soul, just like everyone else we're supposed to be helping."

"The fire changed me too," April said, "but I don't understand how. I'll be honest: whatever is happening to me, I'm afraid of it. I'm hoping Julie might be able to help."

Chris stood, releasing Reese and heading toward the stairs. "I'll dig out Andrew's address for you."

Reese surveyed April. "Do you need someone with you?"

April smiled. Reese asked the question with an aggressive edge to her voice—the warrior coming out. "No, I don't think there's any danger in visiting one of our own. None from Julie, anyway."

Reese hesitated a moment and then said, "I understand . . . what it feels like. To feel like a danger to yourself."

The words made April uncomfortable. "I'm not sure if that's what I feel."

Reese nodded. "I'm here if you need me."

"Thank you."

The offer was bittersweet. April didn't know what she needed, let alone how to communicate it to anyone else.

* * * * *

That evening, April stood on the front step of a suburban

home in a nice, moderate neighbourhood, staring at light pouring through windows—a lot of light, from every window in the house, it seemed—and letting the cold air raise bumps on her skin and give shape to her breath in the air.

"You can do this," she told herself. "You want these answers."

Realizing that if she didn't act quickly she was going to turn and run, she stepped forward and rang the doorbell.

And waited.

It opened.

A pretty woman stood framed in the light. Honey-blonde hair hung in a braid down her back; she wore a rose-coloured sweater and a long skirt.

She didn't look happy—her face fell when she saw who was, or maybe who wasn't, standing on the doorstep.

"Hi," April said. "I'm April. I, um . . ."

"Come in," Julie said, swinging the door open. "I think I know who you are. You are Oneness; I can feel that. So as far as I'm concerned, you're a friend."

"Thank you," April said, still hesitating on the doorstep. Welcome she might be, but she hadn't missed the look on Julie's face when she first saw her, or the unhappiness still evident there. "Are you sure this is a good time?"

Julie smiled at that, but the smile was careworn. "All we have is the present," she said. "Come in, it's freezing out there."

April didn't bother to tell her that she was enjoying the cold—that even though she had always hated chill, now it was reassuring.

Because somehow it kept down the heat inside her.

"Are you expecting someone else?" April blurted out as she entered the front hall and Julie closed the door behind her. "I mean, you looked like . . ."

"My husband went out early this morning," Julie said. "He hasn't come back yet."

"I'm sorry," April said, and then wondered if that was a stupid thing to say. "When were you expecting him?"

"I wish I knew." Julie smiled again, bleakly, and motioned toward the living room. "Come have a seat. I'll see if I can find where Andrew keeps anything warm to drink so I can offer you something."

"You are Julie, right?"

"Oh, yes." Julie gave a short laugh. "Of course I am. I just assumed . . . I'm sorry. I'm distracted. Do you want to tell me why you're here?"

This time it was April's turn to laugh. "Because I want to talk to you, actually. The village cell sends warmest greetings and an invitation to come and see us anytime. Everyone has been wondering about you and hoping you're doing well."

Julie's eyes flicked away, into the house with its many lights on, and sighed. "I hope I can answer that better later." She looked back at April. "I'm doing better than I ever have. And I'm hurting badly. Does that answer the question?"

"Maybe it does. Can we sit down?"

"Of course."

They went into the living room together, and April sank

into a loveseat while Julie sat in an armchair across from it, under a lamp.

"Something happened to you," April began. "And I wondered—I hoped—you could tell me about it."

Julie was regarding April closely—uncomfortably so. She shifted on the loveseat and tried not to clear her throat and make it obvious how scrutinized she felt. Julie took a long time to answer, making the awkwardness even worse.

Finally she said, "I think I'm not the only one something happened to."

"The fire happened to me," April said. "But I'm assuming you know about that?"

"The fire is still happening to you," Julie said.

"And you?"

"Right." Julie folded her hands in her lap and looked down, gathering thoughts maybe. Or just reluctant to speak the thoughts she'd already gathered. "I don't know if I have the answers you're going to want to hear. I don't know anything about being raised from the dead, if that's what you want to know. I remember some things, but they're strange, and I don't think they could help anyone else."

"Honestly," April said, "that was what I was hoping you could tell me."

"Maybe you should explain why you decided to come here?" Julie looked hopeful, like they both needed help finding the beginning and this was her best guess for how to do it.

"I thought the Spirit spoke to me," April said. "I was . . . angry. About death, dying. I don't know. I'm not sure why it

Rise   99

affected me the way it did. It's not like I haven't been around death before. It just . . . it rattled me." She didn't add, *And I felt like I was going to burn up from the inside. Just explode. Again.*

"Hmm," Julie said, her tone both sympathetic and waiting.

"And I just asked. The Spirit. What to do about death. And I thought I heard your name."

Julie sat back, surprised. "He sent you to me?"

"Yes." April frowned. "He?"

"What?"

"Why did you call the Spirit 'he'?"

Julie stared down at her hands now, and gave a nervous laugh. "I guess most Oneness don't."

"No. We normally talk about the Spirit as a force . . . not as a person." Although, now that she thought of it, Reese had used the same wording when they last talked.

"Well then. Maybe that's what I'm supposed to tell you." Julie's face changed as she spoke, becoming a mask of unhappiness. She looked like she wanted to break down, but she held her shoulders rigidly straight and kept her hands clasped in front of her. "When I came to life again, I encountered the Spirit. And he is a person. And he is still with me. And I think . . . please, understand me. I know I'm new. I know I've only been Oneness for a tiny little bit of time, and I know that before that, I let myself be deceived and follow someone who was really evil. I don't think I know everything. I . . ."

"It's okay," April said. She leaned over and laid a hand on Julie's. "It's okay. You didn't choose any of this. I understand. Just . . . what were you going to say?"

Julie's voice shook as she tried hard to hold it steady. "That I think the Oneness has forgotten something really important. That I'm supposed to help us remember. But I don't know how." Tears began to run down her face. "I came here to find Andrew, my husband, and try to make things right between us. I wronged him so much, and he's been so patient, and so good. I hoped he would come into the Oneness when he saw the truth—felt it. But I tried to tell him, and I drove him away."

"That's why he left this morning?"

"He's confused. He doesn't know what to do."

"He isn't the only one," April said.

"Mom?"

A voice, younger than it should have been, interrupted them. Miranda was standing in the living room doorway in a nightgown, clutching a blanket and staring at April. She pointed. "Why is she here?"

"She's visiting, honey," Julie said. "She just came to talk."

Miranda's pointing hand began to shake. "I don't want her here."

April started to stand, slowly. "I'm April," she said. "I don't blame you if you don't remember me . . . I—"

"I'm not stupid," Miranda interrupted. "Of course I remember you." She turned her eyes back to Julie. "Mama, make her leave. Make her go. I don't want her here."

Her voice was beginning to rise, taking on a note of hysteria.

And April was beginning to feel heat.

At first she thought she was blushing—that the awkwardness, the embarrassment of the moment was flushing her cheeks. But it was more than that. It had started in her core, and it was growing, tingling in her fingers and toes, her arms and legs, shortening her breath, brightening her eyes.

She jumped up. "I'll go. I'll leave."

But Julie was staring at her, and she reached out to grab April's arm and pulled her hand back quickly, as though the touch burned.

"No," she whispered. "Stay."

"Mama! Make her leave!"

April's turned her eyes back on Julie, begging. For some reason that she could not explain, Julie's word was holding her here.

"Let me go. I need to leave before . . ."

"Stay. Please."

Miranda's voice rose to a scream. "Mama!"

Another voice—a man's voice—boomed through the house from the direction of the garage, seconds after April registered the sound of a door opening. "Miranda!"

She had no choice.

She ripped herself free of Julie's request and ran.

"What were you thinking?" Andrew shouted. "How could you let her come here when Miranda is like this? Did it even occur to you that she would trigger her trauma? She was there in the fire! Hell, she caused the fire!"

Julie had not moved from the armchair where she'd been seated when April ran. Andrew had gone to Miranda, comforting her, taking her back to bed. He had been with her more than an hour before coming back to the living room, and Julie was still seated in the same place, the same position, hands clasped in her lap, eyes downcast.

"I came back here hoping we could talk. I thought we could make something work. I just don't know now, Julie. I just don't know."

He collapsed into the couch across from her, looking exhausted.

"Where were you all day?" she asked.

"That has nothing to do with anything. Why did you let

that woman in here?"

"She's a friend, Andrew. She saved Miranda's life, as you know perfectly well."

"I know Miranda walked out of the fire holding her hand . . . her and some other woman with them. I don't know anything else."

"You said she caused the fire."

"I don't know why I said that. That's . . . what it seemed like. Like she was the source of it."

"She's full of the Spirit," Julie said.

"What, like you?"

"It's not manifesting in the same way, but yes."

"So this Person living in you is also a raging fire? The kind that killed multiple people and burned a cemetery to ashes? Great."

"Andrew, I'm sorry this isn't simple. I wish it was. But please . . . I want this to work." She swallowed hard. Her eyes were shining. "I thought you weren't coming back."

"I came back for Miranda. She needs me. Obviously."

"I wouldn't have let anyone harm her, Andrew!"

"She was screaming when I came into the house!"

"You're the one who told me she's not okay. She wasn't screaming because there was a real threat."

"That girl looked like a threat to me."

Julie just stared at him. "Then I'm sorry. Maybe we can't make this work."

He shook his head and raked his hair in frustration. "So why was she here?"

"To ask me about resurrection."

"Is that going to happen a lot?"

"I don't know. Maybe. I'll tell people whatever they want to know when they come."

"Great. My wife the freak show."

"Andrew."

He looked up at her, and the pain in her face stopped his heart. "I'm sorry. I don't want it to be like this either. I want to fight for her, Julie. I want to fight for both of you. But right now you look an awful lot like a threat."

"I understand," she whispered.

"I went to my mother's."

"Oh. How is she?"

"Dead. I was at the mausoleum. You used to know my mother was dead, Julie."

This time she laughed. He smiled. What else could he do? What else could either of them do?

She said, "Well. Not all the dead people I know are dead anymore."

He barked with laughter. "Could anyone else on earth give that comeback?"

"I don't know. Andrew, I want you to be with me. I want to be on your side. I want that more than anything. But I can't deny what happened to me, and I can't deny what's living in me now. I can't. It's not a choice."

"I understand," he said. "I really was at the mausoleum. Thinking about all this stuff. Thinking about what you're supposed to do if your wife has been shot to death and resurrected by some power you don't know anything about."

"Did you reach any answers?"

He reached out and took her hand. "I guess you start by thanking that power. Or at least by not assuming it's an enemy. I'm glad you're alive, Julie."

She closed her fingers around his.

* * * * *

On the ground outside the window, shaking with cold but grateful for it, April felt the change in the atmosphere and smiled, her lips tight together against the frost gathering around them. She'd stayed, shaking as much with fear as with cold as Andrew shouted and the shouts played across her memories like a broken instrument. Stayed because she couldn't leave Julie alone with a man who was so angry. Because she knew what that was like. Because someone needed to be there to intervene if that was necessary.

And because she still needed answers she didn't have.

Had she, as she'd heard Andrew say, caused the fire?

It had begun in her.

She had prayed . . . in the place of peace she'd remained in since encountering the Spirit in the deep of the waters in the bay, she had lifted her head with confident courage and asked the

Spirit to come. And he had come—as fire. Beginning deep inside her, and bursting out from her to consume the cemetery and the enemies of the Oneness. She had felt it as power and life, and she had taken Miranda's hand—and Teresa's, she remembered—and stepped out through the fire still burning with confidence, with courage, and with peace.

Where was that peace now?

Why had the fire turned her from confidence in the Spirit to fear of it? How had she become a stranger to herself, to the Oneness, and to the Spirit who gave them life?

She admitted to herself, there in the cold, that she was terrified the fire would break out again. It kept trying. The growing heat, the passionate response—to things like death. And to whatever was wrong with Miranda. And every time she had done all in her power to keep it down, snuff it out, stop it from happening. Control it somehow.

But what else was she supposed to do?

She knew, from her childhood, what it was like to be out of control. What happened when violence simply broke out and raged on. The Spirit, through the Oneness, was supposed to be her shelter from all of that. Not a repeat of it—a repeat ten thousand times worse than the childhood nightmare could possibly have been, because her nightmare had been a relatively private one, and the Spirit filled the whole universe.

The heat had died far down now, and snow was drifting in the air—it was getting too cold to keep sitting here. Wishing the couple inside the house luck, she rose and headed for the street where she had parked Richard's car. She was fairly sure Andrew and Julie really loved each other. That they weren't like her parents had been, even if tonight's fight had been ugly and loud. The little she knew of their lives told her that their love should have ended long ago, but it had not; it had survived all that was thrown at it.

She hoped it would survive this too.

* * * * *

When the plague at last had worn itself out and the countryside began to heal, to rebuild, and to live again, the death toll was devastating. Every family had lost some of their own, the elderly and the children proving especially vulnerable. The abbey in Via del Sol was far from immune; they had lost nearly half their sisters in the final count.

But when they looked back, not one of the sisters felt that death had truly won. At the last, the victories outweighed the losses—or at least proved that death was not the only force in the world that required reckoning with. More than two hundred children who came to their doors in the year that the abbey functioned as a hospital survived. Of these, many had lost their families and did not go home again; most became One. They spread out and formed smaller communities throughout the country, ministering to the villagers and country folk who were still just trying to regain their feet and their hearts after the end of their world as they had known it.

Carmela lived, though she lost her eyesight—a consequence of high fevers that Teresa was not able to bring down.

The last thing she saw, she told Teresa, was that first painting of the Spirit. The one Teresa had done in the midnight hour when Niccolo lay at death's door. "It is my comfort," she told Teresa often. "It lies before my eyes always. A vision that gives me joy and strength."

"I would that it had given you healing also," Teresa answered as they sat together in the garden under a warm spring sun, amidst lush new growth that Teresa could see and Carmela could not.

"Who is to say it did not? I feel as one whose life has been snatched from the door of the netherworld and given back to her. Perhaps this vision had a part in doing that."

Even a greater grief, however, was that Niccolo had stopped painting. Teresa tried to convince him to take up the art again, but "I have lost my heart for it," he told her, and that was the end of the argument.

Ten years passed and Niccolo became a young man, handsome and strong, a servant to all. He travelled the countryside and joined the various Oneness communities as long as he liked until wanderlust took him again. Everywhere he went he was a favourite, and Teresa heard tales of the wonderful things he did.

But things were not right if he was not painting.

She had never forgotten her dream. Niccolo had a great purpose, a heroic one. But he would not reach it if he did not take up the brush again. Of that she was certain.

One more grief equalled that, and it stayed settled in Teresa's heart where she spoke of it to no one: that Franz Bertoller had been driven from their presence a lost man, unredeemed, and she had never done anything to help him. The look in his eyes had never ceased to haunt her.

So when his message came, her heart was more ready than it should have been to receive it. They had unfinished business, her soul and his. And she was frustrated by her lack of impact on Niccolo, who was meant to learn her gift and take it to far greater heights and who instead spent his time riding horseback from place to place, being a charmer and a favourite and making everyone happy but her.

Mother Isabel might have told her to turn the request down, to respond to Bertoller's message with a polite refusal. But Mother was gone too, quietly succumbed to old age a year hence.

His message was short.

> I regret to write that the plague has come to my own country. I have not forgotten the efficacy of your work in combating it. At present I have made of my home a hospital much like the one you once tended at the abbey. Help is lacking. I request your presence to show us the way, to tend to the dying, and to paint visions that heal.
>
> Yours as ever,
> Franz Bertoller

He included none of the appellations of nobility, and that simplicity was the final thing to make up her mind.

In any case, even if she could refuse him, how could she refuse the dying?

She began to make preparations almost immediately. The journey would take ten days by horse; she would ride as quickly as possible, sheltering for the nights with the Oneness cells along the way. Preparations took longer than they should have, perhaps—she did not admit to herself that she was stalling, though inwardly she knew it.

Niccolo was out on one of his journeys, and she hoped to convince him to come along.

To revive the gift she knew he still had.

To help the dream on to fulfilment.

He had been gone some time; surely he would come home soon. The bond between them was still strong; though at times she thought he kicked against it, he always came home eventually. And Teresa knew that she was the real reason he did.

Four days passed, and she knew she could not continue to delay. She had run out excuses to linger. She stood in the abbey looking out over the looping road as the sun set and the moon rose in the sky, deciding in her heart to leave come morning's light.

"Just a little faster, Niccolo," she said to the road. "Ride just a little faster, and you will go with me."

But he did not come.

And she could not keep the lord in his foreign country waiting any longer, nor the dying in his house.

* * * * *

Andrew picked up the phone and hung it up again three times before he finally dialed and sat waiting, clutching the phone to his ear. He breathed out, trying to calm himself as he twisted the curled cord around one hand.

The phone rang only twice before someone picked it up. "Dr. Clancy's office," said a professional female voice.

"Er, yes," Andrew said, "I'm calling about making an appointment."

"Are you already a client here?" asked the voice.

"No, I . . . I'm not calling for me. For my daughter."

"Is she over the age of eighteen, sir?"

"No. No, she's just fifteen."

The voice was unflappable, even as Andrew stumbled over his words and felt like a fool. "May I have your name, sir?"

"Andrew Hunter."

"And your daughter's name?"

"Miranda. Miranda Hunter."

"All meetings with the doctor are confidential. But can you give me a reason why you want your daughter to come in for counselling?"

He cleared his throat. "Your ad in the Yellow Pages said Dr. Clancy specializes in trauma counselling. My daughter's been traumatized."

"Under what circumstances, sir?"

He turned that over in his head. Where to start? There was the cult . . . she had grown up under Jacob's strict rule. Who knew what all had gone on there. Julie had told him a little bit about the man named Clint who had come in and introduced some kind of witchcraft to the community. And the Oneness—he didn't know all the factors there either; how the Oneness had gotten involved with the community and what Miranda had seen or heard. He did know a man had been killed and Julie had been, for a little while at least, a suspect. She was still involved in the court case. And of course, Julie herself had been shot—and then resurrected. And Miranda had hitchhiked back to the community and been picked up by Chris, and then had nearly been killed by a madman as a sacrifice. And then she had walked out through an incredible blaze holding the hands of a woman who was on fire and another woman who, according to his memory, was a ghost.

Oh, and she'd also been introduced to her father for the first time in her fifteen years of life.

"I'm sorry," he mumbled into the phone.

"What was that, sir?"

"I'm sorry." He cleared his throat. "This was a bad idea. I don't think you can help us."

He hung up. Hung his head in his hands. Raked his fingers through his hair.

This was too big.

Just too big. Too much. Too many factors he didn't know how to begin to explain, let alone tackle. Really, it was no wonder Miranda was regressing and acting like a kindergartener. He would too if he were her age.

Shoot, he almost wanted to now.

Two answers presented themselves, and he didn't want to look at either of them closely.

Julie was upstairs, taking a very long time about getting a shower. Miranda was at school. Calling a psychologist had been a dumb idea, but for a few minutes it had sounded like a way to make something of a start.

Rise   **113**

The trouble was, he realized, that psychologists only knew how to deal with human minds and emotions, and so much more than that was involved here.

Two answers.

One, call Chris. Sit down with the young man whose phone call had brought Andrew back into his daughter's life in the first place and ask him for help, even though he was Oneness and his "help" was going to take him deeper than ever.

Two, try to somehow make contact with the Person who was apparently living inside of Julie.

Go straight to the root of the whole problem, essentially.

He laughed out loud at the idea.

Calling Chris might well lead to the same end, but at least the Oneness were human. Or they started out that way, anyway.

A voice in the back of his mind reminded him that Julie was also Oneness. True, he answered, but at the moment communication with Julie was a little strained, and anyway . . . she was different.

That was why April had come here. Because Julie wasn't just like the rest of them.

He wondered if, when the words "for better or for worse" were written into traditional marriage vows, the powers that be had had any concept of what cults and charismatic leaders and killers and demons and spirits could do to a marriage.

"I've hung in there this far," he muttered. "What's a little more crazy in the grand scheme of things?"

Upstairs, he heard the shower shut off, quieting the noise of the pipes in the walls. He wondered what she'd been doing for the last forty-five minutes. Julie had never been high maintenance—well, not fifteen years ago, at least. She probably relished the time shut away from him to think. Maybe pray. Or whatever it was she did.

His hand was resting on the phone.

He picked it up and dialed another number.

There was no sense in pretending this whole situation was just a normal part of human experience, just a bump in the road that time and mutual effort could get them over. He needed help.

The Oneness was the only place he could think of to ask for it.

* * * * *

Julie came downstairs with her hair wrapped in a towel, her whole body still relaxed and her limbs heavy from the coma-inducing effects of the hot water. She couldn't remember the last time she had just luxuriated in a shower like that. The community had drawn its water from its own well and heated it using precious energy produced mainly from their own windmills and solar panels—and frugality was a virtue in all things.

She could hear Andrew talking in the kitchen and drew close to the door, curious.

She felt love swell in her eyes as she anticipated seeing him. Love and gratitude. He was a good man. He was doing so much for them. She could hear the near-desperate tone in his voice, the humility—it only took her a moment to realize who he was talking to. That he would go to the Oneness and ask for help moved her heart. And gave her hope.

Maybe, after all, Andrew would become One.

And then, maybe, he would learn what the Spirit was. Would share her passion. Would help her figure things out.

Maybe.

But there was a hardness in his tone, too, a defensive wall she'd felt every time she tried to talk to him about these things. And she knew there was no guarantee the hardness would change.

Sometimes, increasing pressure only made hard things even harder. Sometimes, adversity made hearts impenetrable.

"Please, Spirit," she whispered.

And she let the Spirit interpret the request.

"Can you hold on?" she heard Andrew say. "There's a call coming in."

She stepped into the kitchen doorway as he said, "Hello?"

His face went white.

She reached for the door frame to steady herself as his words made clear what the person on the other end had said. The conversion was hurried, and it ended with Andrew already halfway to the door, hanging the phone up as he grabbed his coat and keys.

He didn't have to say the words, but he did.

"She's gone. Miranda's gone. They said she ran away."

Reese sat up straighter as Chris hung up, brow furrowed.

"What's wrong?"

"I'm not sure. He had to get off the line, but then he just hung up on me . . . I think something's up."

He jumped on the phone when it rang again. The conversation was short. And Reese could already feel her sword forming in her hand in response to what she sensed before Chris got off.

"Miranda's gone," Chris said. "Her school said she ran away. Andrew and Julie are going after her."

"With our help," Reese said.

Chris smiled, locking eyes with her. "Of course."

She held up her sword, fully formed in her hand. "Don't have to tell me twice."

Chris raised his eyebrows. "You're expecting demons?"

There was a hardness in Reese's voice. "Julie and Miranda

Rise   117

lived in their presence. They don't let go easy. Julie may be out of their reach, but unless Miranda has Joined, she isn't."

Chris had his car started in minutes, and Reese climbed in, slamming the door after her. She could see her breath on the frigid air, but she just rubbed her gloved hands together and breathed into them, cranking up the heat without a word of complaint.

Chris looked over at her as he threw the truck into gear and started down the long driveway of the cottage where he and Tyler still lived, apart from the rest of the Oneness cell. Since his Joining, the little house high on the cliff had become an open residence, a place where any of the village cell were likely to be found . . . just as Chris and Tyler spent much of their time at the main cell house. But the cottage was special to them both, and neither had wanted to leave it completely. Reese was looking out the window, her legs drawn up under her. She looked expectant—even excited.

He had almost forgotten he was marrying a warrior.

Reese had grown up in the cell in Lincoln, where warfare with the demonic was a way of life as it was not in the fishing village. She had been gifted from the beginning with the sword and in battle strategy and skill; she had led attacks, fought harrowing battles, and sent demons fleeing for their lives.

He hadn't realized until now that she missed it.

* * * * *

The meeting with the principal and Miranda's home room

teacher was brief. Andrew wanted out as fast as possible—out so he could get on with the search for his daughter. They were little to no help. The teacher made a few snide remarks about Miranda's immaturity and distractibility; Andrew cut her off. He could tell her a whole lot more about all that than she wanted to know.

"Just tell me where she might have gone, please. Or at least where you think she left from."

The teacher and principal exchanged a look. "We have no idea where she might have gone," the teacher confessed. Andrew couldn't remember her name and didn't ask again. Normally he was polite and well-mannered; today any such attention to details was a waste of time.

"Where was she last seen?" Andrew pressed.

"She came to class after lunch," the teacher said. "She asked to go to the bathroom and didn't come back."

"Great. And no one saw her?"

"We called you when I realized she wasn't coming back."

"And that was . . ."

"An hour later."

He looked helplessly at Julie. "Any idea where she would have gone?"

Julie shook her head. "I don't know anything about her life here. I tried to ask her about school, but she just talked about her friends . . ."

"Her friends," Andrew said. "Can we talk to her friends?"

The principal frowned. "Frankly, I find that a little intrusive.

If you're having trouble at home, that isn't their problem."

"This isn't about trouble at home. She could be in a lot of trouble."

"If you want my opinion, you should get your daughter in for counselling," the principal said.

Andrew glared at him. You have no idea, he thought. None. Out loud he said, "We have to find her first. Can you give us access to her friends, please? We just need something to go on."

He glanced over at Julie. She was frowning. A frown that went deep and bothered him. He cursed inwardly, wishing these people would just give him some kind of answer so he could get his wife out of here and ask what was going on.

Or maybe he didn't need answers from them.

Maybe they truly could not help.

The teacher was talking. Saying yes? Offering help? He tried to shake away the distraction and listen to her. It didn't work.

"Excuse me," he said. "Just . . . excuse me a minute."

He grabbed Julie's arm and steered her out of the principal's office, practically shutting the door in the faces of the confused faculty.

"What's going on?" he said.

"There's something wrong here."

"Yes, there is. Miranda's missing." He forced his tone into a gentler vein. "Julie, what is it?"

"I'm not really sure. But something . . . I don't trust them." She pointed at the office door.

"Is it demons?"

"Not exactly. But there's some kind of threat, Andrew—something very real." She was starting to shake. "It's familiar. Feels almost like . . . like Jacob's here. I can't tell you exactly."

Andrew released his hold on her arm and leaned against the door. "Do you think Miranda could feel it too?"

Julie looked up, her eyes lighting. "Maybe."

"And that's why she ran."

"I would guess."

"So she would go . . ."

"Home," Julie said. "She would go home. I'm sure she would. I can't imagine her just taking off on her own. I mean, she did that once, but . . ."

Her voice faded, and colour drained from her face. "She did that once. When I disappeared, she went back to the community."

"She wouldn't try to go back there now?"

"No, it's not that. It's how she got there. She hitchhiked. Andrew, she hitchhiked."

He stood up straight. "You think she did it again?"

"Does she know how to get to your house?"

"I doubt it. She's been so . . . childlike. Out of it."

"But she knows your address."

"I drilled it into her the first day."

"That's it then. How in the world are we going to find her?"

"Maybe she was picked up by someone who will really just take her home."

They stared at each other.

"Not everyone is a predator," Julie said weakly.

Andrew didn't answer. Didn't voice all the things shouting in his head, the things he wanted to shout at her.

Not everyone has enemies. Enemies that are not even visible to most of the world.

Not everyone is at the centre of something so big it could reshape the world—something bigger than life and death.

Not everyone has you for a mother.

He forced himself to turn around and start walking away, toward the doors. His voice was tight, but he forced the invitation out—"Come on."

He finished the speech in his head. Directed it at himself this time. And not everyone has you for a father. Not everyone is being looked after. Not everyone is loved.

You're going to find her, he told himself. Save her from herself and from all this insanity.

You have to.

* * * * *

"Pull over," Reese said, suddenly and without warning, as Chris idled the truck at a red light on the outskirts of Lincoln. The corner boasted a little store with barred windows covered in tattered posters and cigarette ads; on the other side, a newspaper box and mailbox fronted an empty lot.

"What?"

"The corner store—pull in."

He did. "Reese, what's . . ."

She was already getting out. "Back me up," she called over her shoulder, and in the next instant she had gone into the store.

Swearing, Chris parked the truck and turned it off, yanking the keys out of the ignition. "Can't even wait two sec—"

His muttering cut itself off as he realized a sword was forming in his hand.

Unlike Reese, he couldn't make the thing materialize at will.

This was a response to the presence of the enemy.

Demons.

He walked in to find a sputtering store owner staring at Reese, who stood directly behind a young man in a leather jacket who had slumped to his knees on the floor. His head leaned against the counter; a gun dangled loosely in one hand.

"He must have had some kind of attack," Reese was saying. She was trying to hold the young man up, and Chris rushed to her side and grabbed him under the arms. He maneuvered the kid around and leaned him back against the counter. The store owner was rushing around to join them.

"He was going to rob me," the owner jabbered, "and then this young lady come up and he just collapsed like that . . ."

"It's okay," Chris said, not sure what he was trying to assure the man of. "It's all right. Like she said . . . he must have had some kind of spell."

Reese had gone very quiet, and Chris turned to regard her. She was staring at the kid.

"What?"

Reese motioned toward him with her head. "You don't recognize him?"

Chris looked back and took in the robber's face for the first time.

Of course he recognized him.

Alex.

The teenage boy who had been in cahoots with Clint—Bertoller—and David and the rest of the hive.

Reese's eyes were filling with tears. Chris had no idea why. He turned back to the store owner. "You probably want to call the police," he said, "and file a—"

"Actually," Reese interrupted, "since no harm is done, do you mind if we just take him with us?"

The store owner looked at her like she'd grown a second head. "What?"

Chris echoed the sentiment and the word. "What?"

"I know what I'm doing," she said quietly. More loudly, she said, "He's a friend . . . of a friend. He's sick. You can see that . . . this spell. Seizures. There's no harm done, right?"

Her argument had been less than coherent, but the store owner looked like he just wanted the whole situation out of his hair.

"You get him out of here, and he don't come back, I'm happy." He narrowed his eyes at Reese. "Seems to me you gave him that seizure."

"No, no," she said, already reaching for Alex's shoulder as though she would help Chris lift him. "I just had . . . really good timing."

Chris nudged her aside and picked Alex up himself, holding him under both arms and dragging him out to the truck. He waited until the teen was buckled into the backseat and Reese was seated beside him again before speaking.

"Well?" he said.

"Well what?"

"What's this all about?"

"I felt something up when we stopped at the light, so I went in and found a robbery in process."

"And you kicked the demons out?"

"Stabbed him in the back."

"Reese, why is he in our car? Why is he not in the back of a police car on his way back to juvie?"

She sighed and glanced back at the unconscious boy. "Because it worked this time. And that means he wants to be free."

"Come again?"

She nodded in the direction of the ignition. "You can start the car. I can tell you while we drive."

"Oh, yeah. I almost forgot we were on a mission."

"This didn't happen by accident, Chris. The timing. It's part of the Spirit's plan."

Chris grumbled, but he didn't argue. Compared to Reese,

he had been One for the equivalent of five minutes. She was far and away the expert. He started the truck and pulled back into the road, but said, "So keep talking."

"Last time I tried to drive the demonic out of this same kid, he was holding on so tightly it almost killed him. I almost killed him. Your mother had to stop me." Reese took a second to gain control of her voice—it was clear the memory was a difficult one. "But this time the thing released immediately. It means he doesn't want them anymore. He's tired of their control. Wants to be free."

"He is free, right?" Chris asked, looking in the rearview mirror at their unconscious passenger. "You got them out?"

"It's not that simple. They'll come back unless he fills that space with something else."

"The Spirit."

"Right. He has to become One, or he isn't going to stay free. And isn't really free now—he's just getting a reprieve."

"Isn't it normally messy? When you drive the demons out with your sword and everything? I mean, what I remember from those battles you fought is a lot of screaming and weird clouds and slime and . . ."

"This one was quiet. It's not always the same."

"Right." Chris glanced down at the address Andrew had left him for Miranda's school. They were almost there. But having a passenger changed the picture a little.

"So now what? How do we help Andrew and Julie when we've got Billy the Kid back there?"

"I wish the cell was still here," Reese said.

The Lincoln cell had disbanded a week ago—Tony and Angelica had come by the village to tell them. In the aftermath of David's betrayal and the hive's destruction, they had decided to part ways, the members leaving for other cells and other safe houses. They would regroup eventually, perhaps in quite a different from. But the cell Reese had known as family and home were gone.

"What about Dr. Smith?" Chris said. "Can he help us? Babysit, at least?"

"Maybe," Reese said, "but he's not in town."

"So I guess he's coming with us."

Reese was on her knees, almost turned around completely to face the boy. "Maybe he'll wake up soon."

"What's typical recovery time?"

"Um. 'Typical' doesn't work here."

Chris spotted the school sign on the left and pulled into the parking lot. As he slowed to find a spot, Reese reached out and dug her nails into his arm.

He looked down and opened his mouth to comment before looking back up at her face—and biting back whatever smart-alecky thing had been on the tip of his tongue.

She was staring at the school building with a look that said something was very, very wrong.

"Turn around," she said.

He didn't question, just did what she said.

"That was Miranda's school?" she asked.

"That's the address Andrew gave me."

"No wonder she ran," Reese said.

Chris reflected, briefly, that he had hoped becoming One would mean he wasn't always in the dark about what was really going on. So far, it wasn't helping much.

Except that he could feel Reese's heart as close as his own, and he trusted it completely.

"What did you feel?"

"There's something in that school."

She sat back down, facing forward, and bent her head into her hands, fingers spread across her face. Chris knew that in some way, she was reaching out the Spirit—praying.

They drove another half-mile before Chris asked, quietly, "Are you all right?"

"I'm okay. Where are we going?"

"Well, the school was supposed to be our rendezvous point. But I'm going to guess that Julie didn't like it there any more than you do, and that they aren't there anymore. Plan B was go to their house, and if they weren't back there, Andrew was going to try to leave us a message and tell us where to go. Besides, that will give us a quiet place to wait for our passenger to wake up."

Reese looked behind her again and bit her lip. "I just hope he's more than tired of the demons. I hope he's desperate . . . desperate enough to switch sides."

"What if he isn't?"

"Then you get to see what it's like to lose."

Chris turned down a residential street. "Is that why Jacob's theories were attractive?"

"Partly. It's easier to hate your enemies, even destroy them, than to care about them. It's cleaner."

Chris pondered that as he found the address for Andrew's house and pulled into the driveway. It was nondescript, a typical suburban house in a typical suburban neighbourhood. A family house, he realized. Not a home for a bachelor. And Andrew had lived here for years.

He smiled. "You know something? We could all learn a few things about hope from this Hunter character."

"And about life from his wife," Reese said. She jumped out of the truck and Chris followed suit, heading to the back to remove Alex while Reese rang the doorbell.

No one answered, and Reese tested the door to find that it was open. Chris followed, carrying the still-unconscious Alex over one shoulder like a sack. Reese led the way into the house and pointed to the couch. "You can put him down there."

"Already on my way," Chris said.

A note on the kitchen table said, "No luck at the school— gone to the police station."

"Drat," Reese said. "Why do I think Lieutenant Jackson isn't going to be happy to see us again?"

Chris was about to answer when the sound of someone pulling into the driveway alerted them both that they weren't alone. Andrew walked into the house only seconds later with Julie right behind him. The sight of Reese and Chris startled them, but it was Alex both their eyes riveted on.

"Who is that?" Andrew asked as Julie said, "Is he all right?"

"Not sure yet," Chris said. "Reese drove a demon out of him, and we're waiting for him to wake up."

"I recognize him," Julie said. "He came to the community once. With Clint."

"He was involved with the hive," Reese said. "But I think things have changed . . . he wanted to be free of possession."

Conflict chased across Andrew's face. "Look, I'm grateful to you for coming out, but we need to stay focused on getting Miranda back."

"In my experience," Reese said, "the Spirit has a way of bringing threads together. We ran into Alex—this boy—on the way to find you. I don't think that was coincidence."

Andrew's eyes lit up. "You think he has something to do with Miranda's disappearance?"

"It's possible. Did you learn anything?"

His expression was bleak. "The school couldn't help. She disappeared after asking to go to the bathroom, and they didn't bother to check on her for an hour. We think she probably tried to hitchhike home, but as you can see, she didn't make it back here. We went to the police to file a missing persons report and get them looking for her."

Chris laid a hand on his shoulder. "She's going to be all right," he said.

"You don't know that," Andrew answered, his voice taut.

No one answered him.

"Why hitchiking?" Reese asked.

"Because she's done it before," Chris said. "I found her last time . . . and I told her not to do it again. But I don't think she cared much about what I had to say."

"Why did she run?" Reese asked.

"She's been through so much lately," Julie said. "Too much to process. She's been having nightmares, waking up screaming . . . and there's something at the school. I think something triggered her."

"I felt that too," Reese said.

"I don't know what to do now," Andrew said. "Someone should stay here—man the phone in case she calls. Or the police call with some information. The rest of us—can we go looking for her?"

"That would work if we knew where to start looking," Chris said. He gestured toward the living room. "Right now I wonder if we should just wait for our guest to wake up. Reese may be right. He could be connected to Miranda's disappearance somehow."

Andrew headed for the living room with a grim expression. "Well, let's wake him up."

Chris stopped him with a hand on his arm. "I don't think it's that simple. Just wait."

As if on some invisible cue, the phone rang at the same moment that Alex suddenly convulsed and shouted something incoherent.

All four of them froze momentarily, staring at each other. And then Andrew leaped for the phone and Chris and Reese leaped for Alex.

Chris grabbed the boy's shoulders, holding him steady, while

Reese sat at his feet and looked intently at him. "Alex, it's okay. It's okay. We're not going to hurt you. You're free."

In the kitchen, Andrew's voice was rising on the phone. "What do you mean you can't give me the address? That's my daughter you're talking about!"

Alex's dark eyes stared back at Reese, wide and terrified. She found herself shushing him like an older sister with a child, and he leaned back, trembling, some of the tension easing out of his limbs.

"What's going on? Where am I? Who are you?" he asked.

"My name is Reese," she said. "Don't you recognize me?"

Alex shook his head and then twisted his neck so he could see Chris behind him. He shrank even farther down into the couch. "Who are you?"

"Don't know me either?" Chris asked. "You should."

"I've never seen you before."

Chris raised his eyebrows at Reese. "Is amnesia normal?"

"It is when the demons have been in serious control for a long time. The possessed lose a lot of themselves—lose a lot of their lives."

"What are you talking about?" Alex asked, his voice shaking. It cracked, a remnant of puberty.

"What's the last thing you remember?" Reese asked.

"I don't know, I . . ." He shut his mouth suddenly. His expression went half-sullen, half-scared. "I don't remember anything."

"Except trying to rob the corner store," Reese finished for

him. "It's okay. We got you out of there, and the owner isn't going to report you. Do you know what else happened in that store?"

"I . . . no."

"Do you know what's different?" she asked. This time her voice was gentler—an invitation, an attempt to help him see.

He just stared at her for a long, long minute.

And then he said, "They're gone."

"Yes," Reese said. "We are Oneness—Chris and I. We drove the demons out of you. You're free, Alex. But I would be lying to you if I said you're going to stay that way. They will come back, and they'll come back stronger, unless you Join us."

He shook his head slowly. "I don't want to."

"The Spirit is not like them," Reese said. "The Oneness is not like the hive. Joining is life and freedom. I promise you that."

He shook his head again and pulled himself away from Chris, who was still holding loosely to his shoulders. Swinging his feet to the floor, he stood. His shoulders were hunched, and stringy black hair hung into his face. He seemed to have shrunken since they first encountered him in the store.

"I don't want anything to do with this, okay? Whatever you did to me—thanks, I guess. But I'm just gonna go now. Okay? I'm just gonna go."

He looked up to find Andrew standing in his way, blocking the door out of the living room. "I don't think so," he said. "You're not going anywhere until you answer some questions. What do you know about my daughter?"

Rise   **133**

Chris groaned. "Hunter . . ."

Alex squared his skinny shoulders and tried to keep his head up and look Andrew in the eye. "I don't know what you're talking about. I don't even know who your daughter is."

Andrew shot Reese a glare. "I thought you said he would be connected somehow."

"He is," Reese said, "but—"

"Andrew," Julie interrupted. "They're here."

Another car pulled into the driveway, and Andrew bounded for the front door. Chris leaned over and looked out the window—a police car sat in the driveway, and Miranda was getting out of the back.

Alex, peering out the window, paled.

"Oh," he said. "That's your daughter?"

But Andrew was already outside, talking to the police and keeping an awkward distance from Miranda, who did not look happy to see him.

Chris turned around and pinned Alex with a look. "Well?" he said.

Alex shrugged. "Look, she's just a friend, okay? She's been in trouble; I was just trying to help her out."

"Do you know where she was today?" Reese asked.

He shrugged again. "Probably the same place she always is."

Andrew reentered the house, escorting a miserable-looking Miranda—who immediately spotted Alex and blurted out, "What are you doing here?"

"Ask them," Alex said, pointing to Reese and Chris. Then he nodded toward Andrew. "That your dad?"

Miranda nodded sullenly. Alex cleared his throat. "Yeah, well, I didn't know who your daughter was when you asked me about her. She's just a friend, I swear."

"A friend?" Andrew asked with a dangerous tone to his voice.

"Yes, I keep saying that." He seemed about to say something else, but Miranda shot him a look that they could all read—it very clearly said, "Shut up."

He did.

As Teresa journeyed north, terraced hills and vineyards gave way to wooded foothills and deep valleys. The air turned colder and the inhabitants of the dark more menacing—wolf and bear, raven and demon haunted these forests. She was not afraid. She knew herself to be on the Spirit's mission, and the breath that filled the universe would not lose her to tooth or claw in some forgotten region.

Villages were fewer here as well, and those towns that did exist were smaller and less friendly. She wondered if the hardships of living in the north, the defences required against cold and wild beast and rocky earth, simply hardened men and women against each other as well. Where she could not find pockets of Oneness, she slept alone in the woods, preferring that to the inns encountered along the way. It was late summer, and though the air was brisker here, it was not yet dangerous to sleep out of doors.

She caught her first glimpse of Franz Bertoller's small fortress when she topped a hill and saw it on the crest of the next, across a valley filled with one of the larger towns she had come across since leaving her own country. The house was built of grey stone, walled and defended by parapets and gates—a castle, menacing in its way, and yet promising protection to those who lived encamped around it.

Smoke rose from the hearth fires in the town, and the distant clatter of voices, horses, and activity came with it. She wondered how bad the plague was here, and if she was about to descend into anything as bad as her memories of ten years before. Back then she had thought it was a plague to end the world: that no matter how long she lived, nothing would ever equal it.

The longer she lived, though, the more she realized that life in this world was capable of ending in a thousand ways and yet going on again as something new and different, even as in essentials it stayed the same.

Her horse stamped its foot and snorted, and she patted its neck as it blew out a cloud of cold air. "We're almost there," she said. "Good stabling for you, I hope."

What sort of accommodations awaited her, she could not begin to guess. Nor what sort of greeting the lord of the castle would offer.

She had never forgotten the way he looked at her. That memory had eventually eclipsed all others, though she dimly held those too—the memory of the evil she had seen in him; the memory of his eager fascination with death and dying. All overshadowed by what she had seen in his eyes when he looked at her.

Unexpectedly, she missed Mother Isabel and wished they could have spoken before she undertook this journey. She knew

Mother was a part of the cloud and still connected to her in the Oneness, and she hoped that in some way, the dear old woman oversaw this undertaking and took some active role in it. But how to bridge the gap between them and assure herself of her hopes, she did not know.

Oneness was never ultimately undone by death, and yet death was a terrible thing and a terrible separation all the same.

Nudging her horse, she started down the sloping, rocky road toward the town. On the outskirts, she was greeted by the sight and smell of burning piles of refuse—and to her horror, she recognized bodies stacked in among the garbage.

Yes, death was here.

She averted her eyes and urged her horse forward, though it grew more skittish the further they progressed into the town. The stench was overwhelming—the smoke mingled itself with the unmistakable reek of disease, and that in a town where sewage already ran through the ditches, mingled with mud and rainwater. The activity she had heard from the hilltop slowed and then ceased as she passed, and townspeople turned hard, burned eyes on her as she rode by. She felt the force of those eyes: some regarding her with desperation, some with curiosity, some with hatred, some with lust.

In more ways than one, this town was a cesspool.

It was hard to reconcile the town with her memories of its lord: a clean, well-groomed, confident man who was almost fastidious in his manner and appearance. Somehow she had expected that to be reflected in the people he shepherded; but there was nothing of the manner or appearance of Franz Bertoller here.

Her spirit reached out for some hint of the Oneness present in the crowd, but found nothing. She was alone here.

At least the dying themselves did not appear to be among the townspeople. As she rode past, they turned back to their business, and the clatter went up again—blacksmith, farrier, goods hawker all at work while the dead burned on their borders and the dying lay at their heart.

His letter had stated that his home—the castle—had been converted into a hospital. She wondered who tended the sick. Somehow she had expected to find the Oneness at work alongside the nobleman, but though her spirit still searched ahead of her, she had little expectation now that she would find them once she passed through the castle gates. If they were there, she should feel their presence already.

"State your name and your business," the gruff guard at the castle gate demanded, eyeing her up and down.

She threw back the hood of her cloak and looked the man in the eye. He shrank away from her, though he was twice her size and looked, from the scars on his face, like a man of experience.

"I am Teresa of the Via del Sol, of the Southern Lands," she said. "I have come in answer to the lord's own summons. He requests my help to tend the dying."

The guard looked at her squint-eyed, with a strange mixture of curiosity and fear. "Is that who you are?" he said. "I have orders to admit you. Have you proof that you are who you say you are?"

She reached into her cloak and drew out Franz Bertoller's letter. "I have the lord's request, written by his own hand. And if you should need further proof, the man knows my face."

"Aye, lady," the man said. "That he does."

He waved aside her offer of the letter. "It's enough that you have it in your hand; I believe you. A moment."

With a rattle, the portcullis was drawn up and the low gates opened. Teresa ducked her head as she rode through into a courtyard of surprising breadth, flagged with rough stones. The castle itself stood directly ahead; to her left, stables and a low-roofed blacksmith's shop flanked it, while on the other side stood a chapel. The belltower of the latter drew Teresa's eyes at once; as she dismounted, she searched the simple structure for some sign of life. If a place of prayer had been built here, then surely the Oneness had lived here once, even if they did not now.

A boy took the reins of her horse, and the guard fussed behind her, instructing the lad to take good care of the animal even as he closed the gates again. Teresa was about to turn and ask him a question, but the man who appeared in the entryway of the castle arrested her attention.

He was ten years older, but otherwise the same as he had ever been. Broad shoulders and a handsome jaw, close-cropped hair and fine clothing. His forehead was lined with greater care, and his eyes fixed on her with greater intensity than she remembered.

Such intensity that it stole the breath from her lungs.

He came forward, extending a hand. The few servants and guards in the courtyard moved back as though repelled by the force of his presence.

She reached out, letting him take her hand and kiss it.

"I thank you for answering my summons," he said as he swept a low bow. "So much time has passed that I feared you would not come."

"I had to prepare for the journey," she said. In his presence, in this foreign place so far from home, she was suddenly overwhelmed with what she had done. Why had she come here? What had possessed her to travel all this way to see a man who could only be a threat to her?

A threat . . . because he drew her, attracted her, more than she wanted to admit, and because now that she saw him again, she remembered the evil she had sensed in him. It was still there, vibrant and frightening.

"Come," he said, straightening himself. "You must come and eat and drink and rest. And then I will show you the terrible plague that has stricken my people, and solicit your help in combatting it."

Her first instinct was to refuse the offer of comforts, but she knew immediately she could not do that. She needed the things he offered, and there was nowhere else to turn. Unless . . .

"That chapel," she blurted. "Who built it?"

He looked coolly over at the peaked structure that stood to the right of his stone abode. "It was built by a priest," he said, "a man of the Oneness some fifty years ago. He served my father."

Her heart sank. "He is dead then?"

"Thirty years hence."

"And you have no other of the Oneness here?"

He smiled, a smile that concealed more than it showed. "Indeed, no. They do not often linger in my house. You, in fact, are a special honour to me. You will be the first of the Oneness to reside in my house since my father's day."

She smiled and nodded, and followed him into the castle

with growing trepidation. Once again she wished Niccolo was with her—or at least that he would speed his coming now. That he would come, when he learned where she had gone, she did not doubt. The bond between them had never lessened since his childhood. Yes, he would follow her here.

And then, whatever evil might lurk in this place, they would overcome it together.

* * * * *

Without question, what bothered Andrew most was that Miranda seemed so much older now. It was almost like she had taken off a mask when she left the house, and this time, she hadn't bothered to put it back on. Behind it was someone he didn't know at all—not the scared, immature little girl; not the daughter who adored him and who he hoped to protect and bring up to be a good woman. Instead, the girl who had come home in the back of a police car was a surly teenager whose eyes sparked with hatred and who refused to speak much or to explain anything beyond the absolute facts.

Yes, she had been leaving the school every day. She hated it there. The teachers were "freaks." Something about the place scared her, and she didn't want to stay. Yes, she had found friends off campus and frequented their hangouts. Alex was one of them. As far as Andrew could tell, Miranda's "friends" were a motley crew of high school dropouts and druggies. Every suburban dad's nightmare, in other words.

She refused to talk to Julie at all. Just completely shut her out. Chris and Reese, she treated with so much obvious rancor that they offered to leave only minutes after she came home, and Andrew didn't try to talk them out of it.

He found Julie sitting on the couch in the dark, hugging her knees to herself.

"It's not your fault," he offered.

"Whose fault is it? Yours? You came back into her life just in time to offer her sanctuary. From all the trouble my decisions got her into." She sighed and wiped what he assumed was a tear off her face—he couldn't really see if she had been crying, but it seemed a safe assumption. "This is my fault, Andrew. But thank you for saying otherwise. For all your efforts to work with me."

He sat down gingerly. "We aren't the first people whose teenage daughter has rebelled."

"It's more than rebellion. It's like she's two different people."

"It's trauma too." He paused. "I tried calling a counselor. I thought maybe therapy would help. But I dropped him mid–phone call because honestly, everything Miranda has been through—it's so big. And weird. What can a psychologist know about all this stuff?"

Julie laughed a little in the dark, but it was a hopeless laugh, and it hurt to hear.

"So what's a father to do?" Andrew asked. "Pay a shrink? Move to Alaska? Shoot somebody?"

"At least it doesn't sound like she got into too much trouble with those friends of hers."

"As far as we know. She's barely told us a thing."

Julie's voice wrestled with her words. "I don't know her,

Andrew. And that's my fault too. I tried to be there for her in the community, but everyone was playing such a game . . . trying to be the people Jacob wanted us to be. I'm not sure I've known her for years." A little heat came into her voice, and she leaned forward, out of the darkness into the dim light shining from elsewhere in the house. "Whoever she is, Andrew, there's hope for her . . . but it's in the Oneness. In the Spirit. I know they can help her. I know there is healing there, from everything Jacob did. And . . . from everything I did. And from all the rest of the nightmare."

He fought back the resistance that immediately rose to her words. Because he had to fight it back. Because there was no other answer that he could see.

"She isn't exactly open to the Oneness. You saw how she reacted to Chris and Reese being here. And worse, April. The other night."

"April," Julie repeated. "Andrew . . . I know she won't like it, but maybe she needs to talk to April."

"Why do you say that?"

"You know you've found the right medicine when it starts to interact with the disease. The fire—and the sacrifice, all of it—had to be the highest point of trauma for Miranda. And April was there with her in it. If anyone can help her walk through what happened there and get healing for it, I think it's going to be April."

"Forgive me for saying this," Andrew said slowly, "but is April in any condition to help anyone right now? She looked to me like she could use some assistance herself."

Julie was silent for a moment, and Andrew got the unnerving sense that she was consulting someone else. Then, "I think she can help, Andrew. I'm sure she can."

* * * * *

Melissa was coming home from radiation treatment, and April was keeping as wide a berth from the cell house as she could. Without explaining why, she had moved most of her things up to Chris's cottage and taken up residence on the couch in the long side room with its grungy old shag carpet and its windows that looked over the bay. It was storming out over the water, but the rain had not yet hit the cliffs; she sat on the couch and stared out at it, grateful for the water, for the cold, and for the quiet.

All of those things gave her a sense of security, of stability, as she rested and let herself feel the fire inside.

It was there, burning deep in her core. She could not deny that anymore, and she knew that trying to deny it was a bad road to go down. That it was hurting her to do so. And although she was grateful for the stability afforded by her surroundings at this moment, and though she was assiduously avoiding Melissa and coming into contact with the reality of death, she was also beginning to make peace with the idea that she could not control this fire and was not supposed to.

It was only the beginning of peace. But it was something.

She closed her eyes and let the memory of the darkness wash over her—the darkness in the deep place of the sea, the place that had been in the bay but had not—she knew, with certainty, that she had been transported somewhere else, somewhere that belonged to the world of Spirit and not to this coast at all. She had experienced something there that could not be put into words; it was everything Oneness was, but far more; it was the heart, the personality that had willed the Oneness, with its love and its connectedness and its power that came of unity and community, into being. And it had been working something in that darkness that hid light, creating something—birthing something.

This is the womb, the voice of the Spirit had told her.

The place life comes from.

The birthplace of every great secret and of many things that have never yet been seen or known.

In the confidence and beauty and power of that place, April had walked back into her captors' hands and brought the fiery holiness with her, letting it loose to consume and burn to ashes all that could not withstand its presence.

She trembled, even now, at the memory.

At the time, in the fire, it had not been terrifying. It had exhilarated her. She had been full of the fire and convinced of its rightness. Only after the fact, viewing the ashes, knowing that men had died, and recalling that despite her sense of confidence and power in that moment, she had possessed no control—

Only then had the fear begun to set in, and the desire to keep the fire down. Quench it. Refuse to allow it to break out again.

Somewhere along the way she had ascribed her own father's attributes to the Spirit and assigned the fire that had broken out of her the same motives and ways that had beaten and bruised her childhood and her heart.

But they were not the same.

That was what she contemplated now, here, as she sat alone in the cottage and let herself feel the low burn.

They were not the same.

The Spirit was not her father.

The fire was not one of his rages.

Men had died. But not indiscriminately, and not unjustly. In fact, some men had lived who would not, perhaps, if April had been in control. David had lived. Yes, Reese had shielded him, but the fire had honoured that. And had purified Reese herself, in some sense, without destroying her.

She heard two things in the quiet of the room overlooking the bay.

The first: I am a consuming fire.

And the second: And the bush was on fire, and it was not consumed.

She bowed her head and sank into the heat, letting herself really feel it—the way it tingled in her, the way it warmed her fingers and toes, the way it felt like life and passion.

The same voice that had spoken a moment before spoke again, in that silent way she had come to know was the voice of the Spirit.

You need not fear yourself either, it said.

"Fear myself?" she asked, but she knew the wisdom of those words before she had finished questioning them. Yes, that was much of the problem too. The passion inside—she was terrified to let that loose. Her own passion, not just the Spirit's fire. Her own passionate desire to see Melissa live, and to see wrongs put right. Because she had seen passion before, and so many times it had led to such wrong places.

But you are not those others, the voice said, and you are not walking their road.

"But how do I know I won't walk it? How do I know I won't go wrong if I just let go and trust you and follow this burning?"

Because you'll be trusting me.

"Is that enough?"

Silence met her, but she heard the smile in the silence—the "Of course it is enough."

After another moment of silence:

It is all that is necessary.

"But I can't be trusted," she whispered.

If there was an answer, she could not hear it.

The storm was coming closer to the coastline, and winds were picking up outside.

The voice said, Miranda is coming to see you. She doesn't want to. She wants nothing to do with you. But you must help her see what I have shown you.

April winced, remembering the girl's reaction to her presence in her father's house. The Spirit didn't have to tell her that Miranda wanted nothing to do with her.

They are looking for you at the cell house, the Spirit told her. Go to meet them there.

And she said, "I will."

Teresa passed the night in an ornate, richly furnished room where she felt out of place and intensely uncomfortable, and after sleeping a few hours—she was exhausted, after all—she rose before dawn and found her way through the castle corridors and out to the little chapel.

It was dark within, darker than it should have been, as though someone had long ago extinguished the light there and it had never shone since. She carried a candle from her room, and lighting it, held it up to discover other candles—covered in dust and long, long unused.

Lighting them, she filled the chapel with warm, flickering light.

Candlesticks and censers and other articles of worship lay on side tables and the altar in the front of the chapel, cracked and tarnished with age. But Teresa caught her breath in the living light of the candles: across each of the chapel's four walls, a band of brass had been embedded in the stone. And across it, etched finely and with great artistry, was a depiction of flame—nearly identical to the picture Teresa had painted in her quarters that night so many years ago.

Her eyes filled with tears as the sight awed and humbled her. Not only was she truly not alone in this place, but someone had been here before her who shared her vision and calling—to make the invisible visible. To bring healing and truth in the darkest of places.

When she had finished lighting every candle she could find and the whole chapel glowed with the soft orange light with drew out the etchings in brass and brought life to them, Teresa knelt at the altar and bowed her head, extending her hands before her.

"I am your servant, O Spirit," she prayed. "Let me be a light in the darkness here, as this chapel is a light in the dark hours of the morning. Help me to bring healing, and use my hands and my heart to draw others into the unity that is you—that is your heart."

As she prayed, the awareness of being heard grew strong and convicting—but it was different, this time, than it had been before.

She had often prayed with the conviction that she was heard.

But this time she felt the strong sense of Someone in particular hearing.

Mother Isabel's insistence, all those years ago, that the Spirit should be thought of as a person, even as a man, and not simply as a force or a universal being impressed itself on Teresa's heart, and she felt that she understood it better than she had before.

Because at this moment, in the deepest part of the morning,

the unifying force she had long known as the Spirit felt like an intensely localized, intensely personal presence.

Something about that brought a smile to her lips.

Truly, she was not alone here.

* * * * *

After failing to find her in her quarters, Bertoller cornered Teresa in the corridor outside the eating hall later that morning. "I am surprised to see you out and about so early!" he said. "After your journey, I expected you would sleep for some time."

"I thank you for your hospitality, but I did not come here to sleep," Teresa said. "Though the journey was tiring, I am not accustomed to sleeping the night through. The sisters and I have a custom of rising to pray in the night watches."

"Indeed," Bertoller said, looking her over curiously. His eyes rested on her skirts, where persistently clinging dust showed that she had been kneeling. "Pardon my rudeness in pointing it out, but surely you did not acquire so much decoration in your quarters? I ordered them thoroughly cleaned."

"I felt it was time your old chapel be put back to use," Teresa said. "It is to your credit that you didn't convert it to some other purpose in all of this time."

"I thought to honour my father's memory," Bertoller said, but she was aware as he spoke that some other truth lay behind the chapel's continued existence. She could not imagine what it was and did not care to ask.

"But come," he said, placing a hand to the small of her back. "You must eat. Breakfast awaits."

"Thank you, again, for your hospitality," Teresa said. "But your message indicated your needs were great here. If it is the same to you, I would rather be taken to the sick. I want to see the needs for myself and begin to seek out ways to help them."

Bertoller frowned. "It is not the same to me. You have come a long way; I must insist that your needs be met. You will be little use to any of us if you faint of hunger."

A small smile played on her lips. "We are not so delicate as all that, my lord Bertoller. The sisters often fast, and just as often work hard. The journey has not overwearied me."

"Nevertheless, I insist."

To her displeasure, his insistence won out. A long table in the eating hall had been laid, and she sat at one end and picked at breakfast while he sat at the other and devoured his. The fare was richer than she was used to and heavy in her mouth. This was not why she had come.

At long last, he agreed to lead her to the place where the sick lay. The castle had thus far seemed so close to deserted—haunted only by a few servants of whom she caught the occasional glimpse, and the lord himself—that she had almost begun to think he had lied about the using of it as a hospital. Or about the scope of the plague. Surely there were only a handful of people here.

But now he took up a torch and led her down a flight of stone steps, and as they began their descent, the familiar stench reached her almost immediately, nearly knocking her off her feet—and with it, the sounds of moaning and rustling, the heavy smell of incense, and the voices and movements of workers.

He seemed to notice her astonishment. "The castle is an unusual one," he said. "Much of it was built underground—more than is above ground, in fact. My father had it chiseled out of the stone of the hill where it stands. It is here, you see, that my people bring their ill and their dying."

The stairway they descended was long and narrow, only wide enough to walk one behind the other, but a door at the bottom stood open to an enormous, cavernous room. Torches set on poles burned everywhere, filling the room with eerie light. As at the abbey a decade before, the sick lay on pallets and blankets on the floor, so close together that there was barely room to walk between them. Servants—far too few—moved along the aisles, some bearing water or food. No one was sitting with any of the sick, nor speaking comfortably to them, though Teresa heard harsh tones from a few of the servants. She saw, too, the way they carried themselves—with their faces and noses wrapped in scarves and their arms drawn in, shoulders up and heads back, as though they were trying to avoid the air the dying breathed. She understood instinctively that these had been pressed into service through no choice of their own; their fear of the plague—and their loathing of those who carried it—was palpable.

"Do you have no one else to help you?" she asked in a low voice.

"The townspeople want nothing to do with the sick," Bertoller said. "And we lack any of your kind here."

"My kind," Teresa said, repeating his words almost idly. Her kind. Her kind would come, drawn by compassion and the need to do something about this darkness—about the fracturing that death brought, the reign of corruption that severed all that should hold together. The Oneness held the universe from falling apart. They would be drawn to a place like this with undeniable attraction.

So why were there none here?

Especially when there once had been—when someone had etched visions of the Spirit into the walls of the chapel and lit candles to pray?

"You can see that our needs are great," Bertoller said. "There is a second hall. I believe there are more than six hundred dying here."

"Dying," Teresa said. "And living? Do any recover and go out from here?"

He shook his head. "Not in the three months since I opened my doors."

"Why did you do it?" she asked. "Why not leave them to rot and die in their own homes?"

"The people might have revolted," Bertoller said. "They are afraid and do not want the plague in their midst. By bringing their dead here, I give them a sense of protection and entice them to stay and not flee my land. Besides, I have never forgotten the abbey and what you did there."

The word you was emphasized too much—she recoiled from it. "What we did there," she answered.

He smiled. "Perhaps. But I remember a special power in you. Working through you. I hoped you might bring that power to effect again in my land."

She realized she was staring at him, and she forced her eyes away, down. "I will do what I can. But I will need a few things."

"Whatever I have is at your disposal."

She nodded. "You have clean water?"

"There are wells in the castle courtyard."

"I will need a great deal of water drawn and boiled. And paints—I have brought jars of pigment, but I will need water and binding."

"I have that, and panels and easels. Quite ready for you."

She smiled and nodded again, curt thanks. "Most importantly, I need more of my own brethren. You need the Oneness to fight such a fracturing."

At this, he looked troubled. "As I have already told you, we have none of your kind here."

"There are Oneness everywhere," she said. "There must be some in the countryside who you can call to my aid. Simply put out the word, and they will answer—I am confident of that."

"Very well," he said. "I will send out messengers in search of them."

Once again she felt that his smile and eyes hid something— but once again, she had no wish to pry it out. That his own history with the Oneness went further than his involvement at the abbey was clear, but she would leave that story for him to tell.

"If you will give the order for hot water, then," Teresa said, "and if you would ensure that your servants know to take orders from me, I will see what I can do for your people."

Something in his face twitched, but he did not change expression. "I had hoped you would put your efforts into painting. You need not come down here much at all; it is most unpleasant, and my servants can handle the need."

"No," she said, heat rising in her, "they cannot—they are not. They treat the dying with fear and hatred, as I can see from standing here for only these few minutes; and the day fear and hatred bring healing is the day the world turns inside out. I beg your pardon, but you need great changes here." A little embarrassed at her own outburst, she continued, "I will paint, for that has a part in the healing. But I will not do that first; there are more pressing needs."

He stared at her for a moment before nodding brusquely, turning, and clapping his hands. The servants who walked among the sick stopped and looked up, eyes peering over the scarves wrapped around their noses and mouths.

"Your attention," he said. "I have brought in this lady to direct you. You will obey her orders and serve her every need. Is that clear?"

Teresa raised her own voice on the heels of his. "There will be no need to serve me; I only ask that you serve alongside me. But there is much to be done. We need water drawn and boiled; the filth of this place must be cleansed."

She heard murmurs as several of the servants glanced at each other and muttered responses to her words. She could imagine what they said, but saw no purpose in challenging them here and now.

Niccolo, she thought, why aren't you here with me? I could use your help now.

But she was not alone, she reminded herself. The Spirit was with her—in a strange, intense way she was beginning to realize was new to her. There was something exciting about that.

And, she thought as she surveyed the shuttered eyes of the men and women who would soon begin to work alongside her, the Oneness would join her—if not because she called on those who were already One with her, then perhaps because the Spirit was always drawing others into the unity.

These, too, were encompassed in his plan.

* * * * *

April got back to the cell house just after Andrew and Julie pulled in; she could see them unloading and knocking on the door while she was still a little ways up the street. She didn't bother to hurry her footsteps; the meeting could wait a few more minutes.

Miranda was with them, and even from this distance her body language made it clear she had no desire to be here.

April's heart went out to her. She'd been in that place enough times—forced to be where she didn't want to be. Informed by circumstances and adults and authorities that she had no real say in her own life. Powerless was a terrible feeling; she understood the drive so many teens had to rebel, fight, assert themselves somehow—pretend desperately that they mattered more than they did.

Except that last part wasn't right. Because they did matter. More than they knew. And no human being with a will and a mind was without power.

If only more people realized that.

She couldn't blame most people, though, she realized as she

turned up the walk. She hadn't known anything about the power within herself until she'd been freed from that life, brought into a place of rest and quiet and safety, made One.

Shoot, she was still learning about it.

Snow had lightly dusted the streets, and she stamped it off her boots when she entered the house. Andrew and Julie turned at her entrance; Mary had greeted them, and Miranda was standing with her arms folded in the living room doorway.

"Go on in," April said. "I'll be right there."

She didn't realize until their exchanged glances that no one had actually told her they were there to see her—she only knew that because of the Spirit's word. But she didn't see any reason to explain. Miranda stared at her for a minute and then turned and stalked into the living room, her parents behind her and Mary bringing up the rear with the usual offers of something to eat and drink.

April finished pulling off her boots and straightened up, aware that the heat was tingling again, growing stronger.

And for a crushing, sobering moment, she was aware of death in the house.

She had momentarily forgotten about Melissa.

She could feel the cancer, feel its threat to Melissa and in a way to them all. Mortality like a weight or a stranglehold.

She shook it off. She needed to concentrate on Miranda and her parents.

And to let the fire be—to choose to act on the peace she was making with the Spirit and let the fire be whatever it wanted to be inside her.

She swallowed back a knot of terror and entered the living room. Nick appeared suddenly, out of nowhere like he often did, lingering by her side. She didn't chase him out. No reason to do that yet.

Andrew and Julie had seated themselves awkwardly on the long couch, and Miranda was still standing—at the window, staring out of the living room and completely ignoring everyone else. April could smell cigarette smoke—marijuana, actually—in her clothes and hair. The scared little girl was gone, replaced by someone much older, much harder, and bent on going in a wrong direction.

April had a weird sense that she was looking at herself—the teenager she would have been if the Oneness hadn't happened to her.

Well.

The Oneness could happen to Miranda too.

April bowed her head for a tiny moment to center in on the heat, then raised it again and smiled. "Thanks for coming to see me," she said.

Andrew burst out, "How did you . . ."

"We didn't finish our conversation last time," she assured Andrew, deciding not to explain what the Spirit had just been saying to her. "Anyway, I think it's about time Miranda and I talked about what happened in the cemetery."

She fixed her eyes on the girl's back. "Don't you?"

Miranda answered with silence for a full minute, then slowly and stiffly turned. "I don't want to talk to you."

"Miranda . . ." Andrew started to say, but she glared at him.

"Who gave you a say? You were never even around in my life until a few weeks ago."

This time it was Julie who said her daughter's name, a bit sharply. But Miranda had little grace for her either—though her voice softened when she regarded her.

"Sorry, Mom," she said. "I don't so much trust you either right now."

"I understand," April announced. "I really do. I'd like to talk to you, if you're willing to give me a chance." She looked down at Nick, who was hanging out by her side like a puppy. "Nick, you should go."

He made a half-disappointed, half-annoyed sound, but he exited the scene. Mary was already gone. April rubbed her hands together and met Julie's eye. "Maybe you should go too? Let me talk to her alone for a few minutes?"

Andrew frowned. "Are you sure that's safe?"

He seemed to know the question was strange, and he stuttered, trying to recall it. "I mean . . . I don't know . . ."

"I'm not going to burn anything down," April said. "And I don't think Miranda's going to run. So yes, we should be safe."

But she wondered if she'd spoken too soon. Andrew and Julie had one of those quiet husband-to-wife conferences in front of her, and Julie was already standing to go, and Miranda looked resigned to staying put—

But the heat was intensifying.

She took a deep breath and forced another smile. "Thanks. I appreciate you trusting me. Everything is going to be fine."

She tried hard to hide the trembling of her hands as they left her alone with Miranda.

She'd meant to try to sit and chat and maybe find some common ground.

Instead, the fire was going to break out again.

And she was going to let it.

Andrew cast a nervous glance back over his shoulder as he and Julie moved into the kitchen.

"It's going to be fine," Julie said.

"I wish I believed that."

She took his arm and headed him toward the door. "Let's just go get a drink or something . . . give them some time together. They don't need us lurking in here."

Andrew peered through his glasses at the open, arched doorway to the living room.

A roar of heat nearly knocked him off his feet.

* * * * *

Teresa rolled up her sleeves, grabbed a broom, and started work even before the servants arrived bearing cauldrons of steaming water. In weeks of "tending" to the ill, no one had bothered to clean anything. The hall was past filthy, so bad the smell threatened to knock her unconscious. But she steeled herself and got to it.

At the same time, she got down—lower than any servant had gone in all the time they had been appointed to this terrible place. Down at eye level with the sick. Down where she could take their hands, hear their whispered requests, ask their names, cover them with blankets that had slidden off or remove articles that were sodden and filthy from the effects of disease. The hardest thing was moving on once she had made a connection with any individual—they clung to her hands and skirts and sleeves, begged her to stay with them.

"You are an angel," whispered one old woman.

"No," Teresa said, "I am Oneness. But I am a servant of God all the same. And I am here that you might feel the presence of the Spirit and know that you are not forgotten."

After an hour of moving from one desperate bedside to the next, cleaning as she could, wondering how long exactly it would take until hot water arrived and they could all begin to clean in earnest, she heard a gasping whisper from several rows over and turned to see that one of the aged dying was speaking to someone else—

A servant girl who was leaning over her bedside.

The girl looked up and caught Teresa's eye for a split second, though she quickly ducked her face down again. Long, scraggly red hair framed a face that was all high cheekbones and thin lips.

Teresa smiled. She paused in her ministrations, holding a boy's hand as she watched the servant girl clumsily imitating her own movements, slowly going from patient to patient with an offered hand, a forced smile—a smile that seemed to come easier each time—and a word of kindness.

"Good girl," Teresa said quietly. "You are almost home."

When the water did arrive, it was born by sour-faced servants who gathered in a dutiful huddle to wait for Teresa's orders, but they stood ten feet back, and she could hear their whispers and grumbles—and in some cases saw stiffened backs and a general hardening of skulls—when she announced what she intended for them to do.

"The filth in this place is not fit for animals to live in," she told them. On her orders, several of the women had brought loads of rags, tied with twine, and others held mops and brooms. "Every human being in this room deserves to be treated as a human being until the end, if the end should come—and our hope is that the end will not. Not now."

"Little hope of preventing that," one man said. "They all die."

"This is not the first time I've seen this plague," Teresa said. "That is why your lord called me here to help. In my hometown we faced this ten years ago, and they did not all die. Many did. But many others lived. I charge you to do more than simply contain these people. Serve them. Fight the plague. Quit yourselves like men and women of honour and of war, and let death see that we will not simply let it conquer us without a fight."

They looked at each other, shifting feet, obviously ill at ease. The same man who had contradicted her before said, "Grand fine words. And you are our general, then? And where shall we expect to find you—soaking your pretty feet in your fine quarters while the lord pays you visits?"

Teresa flushed as snickers and outright laughs followed the man's challenge.

But then the redheaded girl stepped forward. "Shut your mouth, Tom," she said. "You've got her wrong. I'll tell you where you'll find her—leading the charge. As she's been doing this past hour."

Another of the women who had remained in the hall while others went after water and rags nodded her assent. "Aye, it's true. The filth on her skirts will attest to that."

Again there was laughter, but Teresa put her embarrassment aside and willfully replaced it with determination. She strode forward, took up an armful of rags, and got to her knees by the closest pallet and patient.

Without a word, she got to work. In moments her brow was hot with sweat and her back aching, and the stench was overwhelming as always, but she set her jaw and kept working.

She was aware that the servants were still standing and watching, but she refused to look up at them.

Someone—likely the redheaded girl—made a bewildered, exasperated sound, and moments later hit her knees across the pallet from Teresa.

Teresa looked up and smiled at her, and this time the girl smiled back.

"Thank you," Teresa mouthed as the others began to disperse, and she heard the sounds of buckets and footsteps and mops hitting the floor, with the slosh of water and a smattering of voices.

"No," the girl said. "It is I should thank you."

168   **Rachel Starr Thomson**

"What is your name?" Teresa asked, relaxing into the conversation as she realized that all the others had dispersed to the corners of the room and were starting at work and conversations of their own.

"I'm called Tildy," the girl said.

"Why did you say you should thank me?"

The girl snorted. "Because I've worked down here three weeks and was like to forget I was a human being, treating these all like cattle as we were."

"It works that way," Teresa said. "We lose our own humanity when we don't see it in others."

"But Miss, surely this is not why the master brought you here? He told us you was coming—but to do grand things. To paint, he said. And work miracles."

Teresa laughed. "Miracles? His memory has grown faulty."

The girl hid a smile at that; Teresa suspected she was not beyond making fun of the lord herself, but she wasn't likely used to doing so in the presence of her betters. If Teresa should be considered a better. Judging from the behaviour of the other servants earlier, she didn't think any of them knew how to classify her.

She wondered how the lord classified her.

He was not happy with the way she had chosen to begin her sojourn with him, that was clear. But he could hardly forbid her from doing what he had asked her here to do. Besides, though he was her host, he was not her liege, and she had no compunction about flaunting his wishes if duty called for it. Duty—to the Spirit, and to the needy before her.

Tildy worked beside her as the hours drew long, never straying far from her side. Though the work was hard and the others groaned and complained in the process of cleansing the hall, Tildy did not—instead, she seemed to soften as the hours slipped by. Her manner toward the ill grew more and more genial and kind, and Teresa watched her with keen interest. She knew what she was seeing—a soul drawn into the Spirit, acting out its response to the Oneness even before it had recognized the call.

As the day drew to a close, Teresa hoped to take the girl aside and speak to her about the influences at work on her heart. Spirit willing, there would soon be a Oneness cell again in this place.

* * * * *

The inferno ceased nearly as suddenly as it had sprung up—before Andrew could think or react, whatever was happening in the living room was over. He rushed back inside to find both April and Miranda on their knees, neither apparently harmed, both in a state something like shock. This was not the cemetery again; nothing was burning, no smell of smoke hung in the air, no ashes marked the remnants of trees or grass or human beings.

But Miranda—

Miranda was different.

She looked up at him and blinked away tears, but she was quiet—no hysteria. No panic or theatrics. And the surly resentment was gone.

"What . . . what just happened here?" he asked.

Miranda shook her head wordlessly and rose, unsteadily, to

her feet. Andrew took her arm and helped her up, then let her lean on him—and wrapped his arms around her as she leaned in close. He held her tightly and looked at April, all his questions in his eyes.

"The Spirit," was all April could say. "It was the Spirit."

And her eyes went to a painting hanging over the fire. Andrew turned to look at it too. It showed the bay that stretched away from the cliffs and the fishing village, blue under a summer sky. But in the sky above the water was something else—a light.

A living light.

And suddenly Mary was in the living room, holding a pot of tea and a tray with two cups, and she was asking them something banal and hospitable—"Milk or sugar?"

She looked from one to the others and quickly set the tray down. "What is it? Did something happen here?"

"Didn't you see it?" Julie asked. "Or hear it?"

"See . . . I'm sorry," Mary said. "I'm not sure what you're talking about." Her eyes rested on Andrew and Miranda. "But it seems that whatever happened, it was for the better?"

"Yes," Andrew said, as he felt Miranda nod her head against his chest. "Yes, I think so."

April was still on her knees.

She looked up, and her eyes settled on a boy sitting in the stairwell that led the bedrooms upstairs. Nick. Wordlessly, he held up a page from a sketchbook, and on it, a hastily drawn sketch of a fire. Filling the living room.

His expression, solemn and almost fearful, turned to a sudden grin.

"So that's what it looked like," he said.

* * * * *

Hours later, April's hands still felt singed. There was no pain—just a remnant tingle, a lingering heat, and a feeling that was half-exhaustion and half-exhilaration.

She'd needed that as badly as Miranda had.

They had both needed to remember exactly what happened in the cemetery.

The deaths, and the police reports and the adjustments, all of that had overshadowed the truth. That the flames had not been primarily destroying, but primarily cleansing, healing, rescuing. They had been personal.

And for them both, the Person in the fire had been a comforter and friend.

Nick finished his sketch, signed it with his initials in big block caps, and stuck it on the refrigerator with a note asking Richard to buy a frame for it. The sight of it made April smile as she sat at the kitchen table across from Miranda. The rest of the house was empty, except for Melissa, who was asleep upstairs. Everyone had decided to give them space.

"I'm not afraid anymore," Miranda said. "It's so strange. I've been scared forever, it seems like. Since way before the fire happened. But now I'm not. Like the fear just got burned right out of me."

April understood. At this moment, it felt as though her emotions were held within a safe enclosure, mind and heart hidden beneath a covering of peace. It had settled over them both, a heavy calm, one that kept every other feeling in check. She could remember the other feelings—uncertainty, fear, the very edge of panic as she let the fire break loose—but could not feel them now. Almost couldn't imagine feeling them ever again.

"But what is it?" Miranda asked. "Can you tell me that? What is the fire?"

"It's an expression," April said. "A . . . manifestation. Of the Spirit."

Miranda frowned. "Like the Oneness?"

"The Spirit and the Oneness aren't the same thing."

"But the Oneness is a manifestation of the Spirit. Like the fire is."

It was true.

Miranda's words, incongruous coming out of a mouth that only hours before had been so sullen, and before that had seemed chronically immature and unable to deal with any kind of reality at all, clicked something into place that April had never, ever understood before.

And suddenly that thing seemed like the most important reality in the world.

"Ye-es," she said. "We are."

And then she asked, "How do you know that?"

Miranda shrugged and looked down. "Jacob used to say it. He said that's why the world was so wicked and bad. Because they were meant to be a manifestation of the Spirit, and they twisted it and perverted it."

"Jacob said that?"

"He wasn't an idiot. Or all bad."

April toned her reaction down. "I'm sorry."

"It's okay." Miranda was quiet for a long minute. "Everybody acts like I should be happy that he died. But I'm not. He wasn't perfect, but he was like a dad to me. The closest thing I had. I hate that everybody just talks about the bad stuff now. Some things he wanted were good."

April didn't interrupt. Miranda needed to talk. Under the calm that had settled over them, she did not grow emotional or choked up, but April could tell the words came from deep within—things Miranda had been dwelling on and hadn't been free to say.

"It's not that easy to just give up your whole life and live a new one. The community was home. I don't really understand why they did some of the things they did. I don't know why Jacob thought it was okay to bring Clint in. Even though I liked him too, at first. And all the stuff he did . . . there was bad stuff. That was when I started getting afraid. He was teaching the men things."

"Some form of witchcraft?" April asked.

"I guess. Stuff like what was happening in the cemetery."

April reached out to lay her hand on Miranda's arm, but the girl manuevered away from her, and April withdrew.

"I just don't know. I don't know what's true anymore. Or who I am."

"The Spirit can help you find that," April said.

"I thought so, when the fire was burning."

"Maybe that's why it broke out—to show you the truth. To invite you in."

Miranda shrugged. "I don't know. I don't know if I can trust it."

"It burned yours fears away."

"But not my questions." She cast her eyes down. "And the fears will be back, maybe."

April wished she could say that wasn't true.

"Miranda," she said slowly, "what you experienced—what you've experienced twice now—it's not usual. Most of the Oneness never encounter the Spirit like that. He's giving you a gift."

Miranda lifted her eyes suddenly. "He?"

"Yes. He."

"My mother calls the Spirit that. She's gotten freaky about it."

"She's encountered him too. Like not many do."

Miranda turned her body so she faced away from April—drawing a door shut. April tried to hide her own frustration and disappointment at the action. How could she still be shutting them out, after what had just happened? While this peace still reigned over them—this Presence that was the embodiment of safety and help?

"So yeah," Miranda said. "What I felt in the fire—it was a person. You felt that too?"

"Yes."

"Why doesn't the Oneness talk about the Spirit like that? Like a real person?"

April wanted to say, We do, but she knew better—they didn't. Not really. They sometimes spoke of "God" or phrased the Spirit rhetorically as a personality, but they thought of him and spoke of him as a force, an unknowable entity, even a kind of unifying principle.

Not as a person.

Not really.

Miranda was growing colder, and her body language showed it. April could feel a distance opening up between them, and wanted to fight it—and felt helpless to do so. She had thought everything was finished when the flame broke out. She thought the Spirit would simply burn away everything in Miranda that was resistant to him, to the Oneness, and that the fire would heal all there was to heal.

I have brought healing, a voice unexpectedly said in the depths of April's heart. But that is not all she needs.

April cocked her head, torn between trying to listen to the voice—to press deeper into the conversation—and trying to hang on to the ever-more tenuous thread of communication with Miranda.

She repeated what she had said before: "The Spirit has given you a gift, Miranda. He's shown himself to you more than to almost anyone else I know. You—"

Miranda interrupted, overriding April's last sentence.

"Maybe I don't want him."

"But . . ." April grasped for words. "But you felt him. Who

he is. You . . ."

"Look, I'm having enough relationship trouble, okay? I don't even know who I am. Or who my parents are. Don't ask me to welcome all this. I'm glad the fear's gone. He helped with that. I'm glad." She stood. "I'm grateful. To you too—thanks for listening to me. I appreciate it."

It was the most words April had ever heard Miranda say all together, and she was left dumbfounded as Miranda left the kitchen, pulled on boots and coat, and headed out the front door. In search of her parents, April assumed.

How?

How could she not want relationship with the Spirit after all that she had seen and heard and felt?

Even after the healing?

But the questions kicked the door open to a flood of others— questions that had been dogging all of them in the months of battle and breakthrough they had walked through. How could David turn against the Oneness, even after knowing the love and community and power they offered? How could Jacob be so right and so wrong at the same time? How could everyone have mistaken Reese's heart as badly as they did, and how could Reese herself have gone so far in the direction of bitterness and revenge as to welcome demons into her company? How could Diane have denied her place in the Oneness for so many years and even hidden their existence from her only son? How?

How could April be so afraid of the fire burning within her?

Even after the encounter beneath the water, in the womb; and even after the cemetery?

She groaned and leaned her head on her hands. Maybe human beings were just a lot more complicated than she thought.

"What does it take?" she asked out loud. "You've done so much for us. You make us One. You hear our prayers. You give to us—heal us. Resurrect us. How can we still turn away from you? And misunderstand you?"

She asked, knowing even as she spoke that she was still guilty of all these things herself. That she had succeeded in making peace with the fire so far as to let it break out in Miranda's presence and do the work it needed to do, but that her fears were far from truly gone—as Miranda had said, they would be back.

"Those are good questions," a voice said.

For a confused second April though the Spirit was answering out loud—but then opened her eyes and lowered her hands, and saw Melissa standing in the doorway.

Melissa's long blonde hair hung in a braid behind her, and she wore a bathrobe and slippers. Her face was pale and haggard, dark circles beneath her eyes.

She padded across the floor and eased herself into the chair across from April.

April tried not to stare. She had been avoiding Melissa ever since the doctor's office. Afraid of what the woman's prognosis might trigger in her.

"Good questions," Melissa said again. "I've asked them myself. I turned traitor to the Oneness when the demons offered me healing. Even used children to help myself. That's ugly." She grimaced. "I'm an artist—a musician. I'm supposed to be sensitive to what is beautiful and to see past appearances to the real meaning of things. I'm supposed to draw all of that out. And yet I went along with a gross lie for all of that time, and the hive nearly had me."

April lowered her eyes and looked at her own hands. It wasn't lost on her that the demonic powers that had tried to woo Melissa to their own side had tried just as hard to kill April—several times over.

Without consciously thinking about it, she had felt superior because of that.

Maybe she still did. After all, the Spirit had taken up residence within her in some frightening, powerful way.

And all that had taken up residence in Melissa was death. Cancer.

"But do you know what I think the answer is?" Melissa asked, oblivious to April's thoughts. "I think the answer is love."

"The Spirit loves us," April said.

"But more than that. We've got to love him too. That's what will hold us, bind us to him. Otherwise we're liable to wander away. All of us."

Even you, a voice within April told her.

And it shut down, and put to shame, all of her thoughts of a moment ago.

No, she wasn't any better than Melissa. Yes, Melissa had tried to save her own life through wrong means. And April had gone running into the cold numerous times in a pathetic attempt to control the power that held the universe together.

She laughed. Melissa regarded her curiously. "What's funny?"

"Not sure I can explain."

Melissa nodded. She rubbed one arm with a long-fingered hand. "You know, I don't think our battle is over. I think we may just be entering the real war. And maybe that's why all of these things are happening now. To you. To Julie."

April frowned. "What do you mean?"

"We need love," Melissa said again. Then she leaned forward, and said intently, "We can't love someone we don't know."

* * * * *

It took Teresa and the servants two days to finish scouring both of the sick halls, work that was considerably slowed by the necessity of simultaneously looking after the sick themselves. This task was made even more demanding in that Teresa actually required it to be done: she gathered, from the comments she heard and the response of those among the ill who were still verbal and conscious, that the care had been only intermittent before her coming, and that some had been lucky if anyone tended to them at all. Tildy continued to work near her, though the hoped-for opportunity to speak with her about the Spirit did not come. They worked until late into the night, and by the time Teresa retired, bleary-eyed and aching in every bone and tendon, Tildy had already disappeared.

By the end of the second day, she had decided that more drastic changes had to be made.

"We must move them," she announced to Franz Bertoller, whom she hunted down after spotting him across the room in the second of the sick halls. It was the first time he had come down since escorting her there on her first day, and he disappeared quickly, but she managed to find the exit he had taken and follow him into an upper chamber.

"I beg your pardon?" he said.

"It is no good, their being underground. The air is intolerable. We must bring them aboveground where they can breathe, and where those who tend them can breathe."

"You had them all in a hall at the abbey," Franz said.

"But the abbey was open to the air!" Teresa said.

"In your country it is warm," Bertoller said. "You can afford to be open to the breezes. But here it grows cold, and we face other threats as well. You do not know what you are asking for."

"It is not cold yet," Teresa said. "Put up tents in the courtyard, if there is nowhere else, where they can be shielded from the extremes of sun and rain. I feel it is needed."

"And yet you have not painted even one picture," Bertoller said, "and in all this time you ignore my wishes in order to crawl around in the muck."

She kept her anger down. "There would be less muck to crawl around in if you would heed my advice, or if you had required your servants to quit themselves as human beings."

"You think this is my fault?" he asked, a dangerous tone creeping into his voice. "May I remind you that no one required me to bring the sick here? That most lords would have left the people in the country and towns to die and be burned in rubbish heaps along the roads, and to dig their own graves while their nobles hid in their castles? I have opened my gates and done more than any noble within a hundred miles would do. Give me some credit."

"I do," she said, her tone genuine. "I do, my lord. But why do something only halfway? I tell you, the air will help them. And will make the work far more tolerable for your servants. You have gone to trouble and expense to bring the sick here. Why not give them a better chance, when there is a way for you to do so? Why let them all die under your doorstep?"

He stared hard at her for a long moment, then nodded. "Very well. I will send you men with the authority and resources to put up your tents. Direct them as you see fit."

"Thank you," she said, inclining her head slightly.

"On one condition."

"And what is that?"

"That you do what I called you here to do—paint." He lowered his voice, softening it. "Though few would do it with such passion, there are hundreds of women who can clean and give orders and tip water into the mouths of the fevered and dying. There are not hundreds of women who can do what you can do—who can paint visions. There is power in that, my lady, just as there may be in fresh air."

She found herself blinking back sudden and entirely unexpected tears.

He might have Mother Isabel, speaking to her.

She received the correction as though he had been.

"I shall," she said. "You are right, and I shall. Only let me get operations in order first. The needs of your people are desperate, and I cannot leave the servants without direction."

"As you say," he said. "I told you I would send you the men you need, and you may direct them. Only do so in such a way that your attention becomes free to divert to your own gift."

She mulled over his words as she descended again and began to share the plans with the servants, alerting them to the change to come. Their expressions ranged from relief to skepticism—often on the same face.

"Do you really think fresh air will make a difference to the sick?" Tildy asked. "My mother always said it would make a body worse, and the wild air should be shut out as much as possible."

"I do think it will," Teresa said. "I cannot tell you why. But in the Oneness, we say that the Spirit is in the wind. I think it will do us all good to be able to feel that wind—the breath of heaven on our faces."

"It will help us all to breathe, that is for certain," Tildy said. "We should thank you for that, even if your ideas are cocked."

She gasped at the end of her sentence as though she knew she ought not to have said it.

"Quite all right," Teresa said with a smile. "You have not offended me."

"You speak of the Oneness," Tildy said slowly.

"It's what you've been feeling," Teresa said, "from the time I came into this house. The Spirit is drawing you into a family, Tildy."

The thin-faced girl trembled. "I do not deny feeling powerful strange ever since you walked in. I've felt like someone hidden in a cave, and you have been calling me out."

"Not me," Teresa said. "The Spirit. God. The powers of

heaven. The Oneness are his people. He makes us a part of each other—a single body, though we are all individuals. He arms us in the struggle against darkness and chaos."

"And disease," Tildy said.

"The very truth."

Trouble haunted her eyes. "Some have talked like you in this land before," she said. "My mother told me of them."

"It's true," Teresa said. "At least one kept the chapel next to the castle, in the elder lord's days."

The trouble deepened. "Aye, the priest. All called him Father, and no other name."

"What happened to him?" Teresa asked.

But at that, something in Tildy's expression closed off. "He died," she said, but her voice strained, and Teresa knew she was lying. "He died as all old men do."

They were interrupted by the arrival of the men Bertoller had promised, both dressed in guards' livery. Tildy vanished while Teresa held conference with them, until at last she was satisfied that preparations were underway to move the sick aboveground and shelter them adequately there.

She cast about for the girl when the men had been dismissed, but the wiry red hair and thin frame were nowhere in sight.

And it was time, Teresa knew, to keep her side of the bargain.

To obey the lord of the castle as she would have Mother Isabel—not, this time, because of any binding vow, but because he was right.

All the old trepidation returned as she made her way to

her quarters. She had argued unsuccessfully with the lord over the choice, wanting to be moved to another chamber that was simpler and not so lavishly furnished. She felt like a pretender where he had placed her—or a mistress.

The latter thought made her feel sick.

She could not paint here, she decided as her feet touched the threshhold of her room. He might force her to sleep in these chambers, but awake, the place would distract her far too much. So she took up panel and easel and paints, as much as she could carry at one time, and made her way out to the chapel.

She nearly bumped into Franz Bertoller himself in the corridor on the way out, but she only mumbled an apology—she was holding several paintbrushes in her mouth—and pushed by him.

In daylight, the chapel was far dustier and less mystical than in the dark hours of the morning. The brass etchings were more visibly tarnished and the altar flecked with brown—mud, she thought. She had noticed it the first night, but it was only barely in the shadows. Even so, the place felt like home. She imagined the cloud were here, invisibly, those who had prayed and worshipped before her cheering her on. A single piece of stained glass, fitted above the altar, glowed blood-red in the daylight.

Laying aside her brushes and dye jars, she set the easel up to face the altar and the shining glass, and she set about cleaning a bit—dusting, de-cobwebbing—while she began to say prayers and to wonder what she would paint.

As a young woman, new to the Oneness and not yet reticent about her gift, she had imagined that in her older years she would be able to paint anything, anytime, and it would always be the perfect thing; years and practice would teach her to skip the awkward blank and lack that always came before trying to make art. That dream had never been realized. If anything, it had gotten harder, and with every successive painting, she felt more and more like she would never be able to do it again. The power evident in her paintings only made that worse; she desired that the Spirit would use them, that he would pour himself through her brush and create objects that truly could, as Bertoller seemed to expect they would, work miracles. But with the exception of that single vision that had painted itself through her at midnight in the abbey, with every new piece of wood she felt like a novice painting some clumsy device all her own. And when, after the fact, they proved to be usable in some way by the Spirit—which they all did—it was a surprise every time.

She did not know how the Spirit did it.

Which made it impossible either to force his hand or to duplicate her own efforts.

She lit candles all around the chapel even though it was daylight—because it felt fitting that they should be lit, and perhaps because she was stalling.

At times, while she put paint on treated wood, she felt the most alive that she ever did.

But this great lump of uncertainty and insecurity and directionlessness beforehand, this made her want to go back to scrubbing the hall floors and daring the mockery of the more surly of the servants. On her hands and knees scouring floors, the humiliation was far more controlled.

"Come, Holy Spirit," she prayed as she lit the last of the candles and turned to her paints, mixing them absently and desiring inspiration to strike. The deeply wooded hills she had come riding through offered possibilities; in their darkness and danger there was yet great beauty.

But then she was mixing yellows and reds, and the form she began to put on the thin panel, almost in spite of herself, was Tildy's face.

She smiled when she realized what she was doing, and when she began to outline high cheekbones and large eyes.

"You're a part of the story now," she said. "And a thing of beauty. Truly."

Something about Tildy's features, here only hinted at, reminded her of Niccolo's, and for a moment her hand faltered. The notion that she ought to paint him, to perhaps speed his way to her and call out to his heart, tempted her.

But no, that was not the way. It was not Niccolo the Spirit wanted in this picture.

She did not know when Bertoller entered, nor how long he had been standing there when she turned to wash her brush and noticed him.

"Oh!"

"I'm sorry to startle you," he said. Without waiting for answer or invitation, he strode forward and peered closely at the painting. "I have seen that face before. One of my servant girls, is it not?"

"One of the best," Teresa said. "She has been my right arm below."

"You will be glad to know progress is being made in the courtyard," Franz Bertoller said. "Soon we shall bring the dying forth for all to see, like a festering secret dragged into the light."

"It is not a flattering simile," Teresa said.

"Nor should it be. The dying are not a pleasant household."

"Yet they are men and women, and children, just like us."

He peered at her. "I am not suggesting otherwise. Forgive me—I think you took my comment in the wrong light. I meant only that what has been hidden will now be made known. No visitor to my house will be able to avoid them, and the plague will be seen for the immense threat that it is. I think, in a way, having them tucked beneath the castle has made it seem less a danger."

"There is danger of its own in that," Teresa observed, "for it is a lie. Little good comes of tucking darkness away; it is like hiding a wound and hoping it will heal itself."

"Wounds sometimes do."

"Perhaps." She picked up her brush again to resume work but found that she could not with him standing there. He was looking around the chapel now, taking in the burning candles and the neatness she had tried to bring to some of the chapel's messier corners.

"I have not seen so much life in this place in many years," he said. "Not since I was a much younger man. But this is not the place I set aside for you. Are your quarters not to your liking?"

"They are too grand for me," Teresa said, "as I have already told you. I am grateful for the honour you pay me, my lord, but I would rather you allowed me to move down with the servants. Or at least to more humble apartments than what you have allotted me. I am not used to it."

"That is a pity," he said, a forced lightness in his tone. He had moved closer to her, and she took a step back, suddenly aware of the small space the chapel afforded and of the fact that they were alone. Remembered danger recalled itself—the young nobleman in her chambers at the abbey, threatening her in manner and word.

Why hadn't Niccolo come?

"Hardly a pity," she said; "I need no more than a simple room and enjoy the life I live."

"Only because you know no better," the lord said. "I confess I hoped to show you a better life here. You turned down my offer, many years ago, to bring you into the royal courts and make something great of your gifts. Those offers are not yet closed to you, though age will soon shut doors."

"The greatest painters are old men," Teresa said.

"Yes," Bertoller said, amused, "old men. For an old woman there is no place to advance. But then, you are still far from being an old woman."

How he moved so fast and so close she didn't know, but she found herself suddenly trapped between the easel and himself. "You are not yet old," he said, his voice lower now, "and you are as beautiful now as you were a decade ago."

"Step aside, I beg you," she said. She straightened her shoulders. "No, indeed, I command you. I am not your subject, Franz Bertoller; I tell you, step aside."

He raised his eyebrows, but to her immense relief, he did as she said. She removed herself from the trap and stood ready to flee out the door.

But his manner had changed—the threat was gone. She almost thought she had imagined it. His eyes turned back to the canvas, and he said, "Though I might question your choice of subject, I see you have lost none of your skill—even none of your magic. I will leave you to your work, in whatever place you choose to practice it. I am eager to witness the results."

So, she had to admit, was she.

Andrew came down early intending to go for a run through the neighbourhood. He needed to work off steam. Besides, all the trouble lately had him way off his routine. If he didn't get himself back in shape, before he knew he wouldn't just be a normal suburban father dealing with suburban teen problems, he'd also be fat.

He had moved back upstairs after Julie decided to move in with Miranda—neither of the girls felt it was right that he keep sleeping on the couch.

He moved quietly through the house, not wanting to wake them up. He wasn't expecting to find Julie already awake.

She had positioned herself by the lamp in the living room, and she was on her knees, praying.

At first he assumed she had heard him, and he was going to apologize, but then he realized she was more intently focused than he'd given her credit for. She didn't know he was there.

For some reason he stood there and watched her, overcoming his initial desire to interrupt and finding it quickly replaced by a fascination that surprised him and held him riveted to the floor.

This was it right here. The heart of all the trouble. Of everything that had changed his life. Julie and her faith.

Fifteen years ago, the faith had been badly misplaced.

This time, he had to admit he didn't think it was.

The power that lived in Julie was real. There was no point in even trying to deny that. It had raised her from the dead. It had killed others in the cemetery. He had seen it blazing with his own eyes. And it had helped Miranda through April—even though his daughter was still doing things her own way, the encounter she'd had with April had broken through something that had not come back.

So the question wasn't whether Julie's faith was a lie. This was real. The question had to be whether the object of her faith this time was good or not.

And he still wasn't sure he could answer that question.

But standing here watching Julie in the lamplight, he knew with a hard knowing that it was good for her. That this place of faith was the right place for her to be—that she was home. That she was loved. That something was working in her he didn't understand but had to honour.

Quietly, he slipped away from the living room door and headed out into the cold to run. But what began as a jog, on the frosted sidewalk, soon slowed to a walk. Stars shone overhead, twinkling above the streetlights. He found himself staring up, pondering the sky, wondering about this world he lived in. Where it had come from. What it all meant. He blew out breath in the frosty air and thought about life and the air in his lungs. He wondered what a soul was and what his looked like, and Julie's and Miranda's. These women who were the most important thing in the world to him, and yet he barely knew them.

He wondered if a lifetime would be enough to know them, or if they would always be strangers to a degree.

Eventually his thoughts forced him to the other Presence, the fourth personality in the house. Julie's God.

The only one residing in his home whom he did not know at all.

He was weighing several conflicted thoughts about that when he saw movement across the street and realized, after a moment, that he was watching someone break into a house.

The crook, dressed in black, with one leg through an open window, paused and looked back to scan the street. He disappeared into the house a moment later, and Andrew didn't think he'd been seen.

But he knew that face. It was the kid Miranda had been with.

Alex.

He stood frozen in indecision for a moment. Call the cops? Try to wake up the owners of the house, assuming they were even there?

He found himself jogging across the street to do the most unreasonable of the options that presented themselves: try to stop Alex himself.

The window sill was high enough that Andrew had to hoist himself up, but it wasn't hard to do.

"Psst," he stage-whispered. "Alex. Alex, where are you?"

His eyes worked hard to adjust to the gloom, and in a second or two he made out the teen's thin shape standing across from the window. Totally still. Staring at him.

Andrew hoisted himself higher so his frame filled the window. "It's Miranda's dad," he said, whispering even more loudly. "I saw you break in here. Listen, I won't call the cops. Just get out of here now and everything will be fine."

"Get out," the boy whispered.

"I'm not leaving without you," Andrew said. "You come, there won't be any trouble. I just want to keep you out of jail this once."

"Get out," the boy whispered again. His voice was barely audible in the darkness.

Andrew wedged his shoulder against the window. His arms were getting tired. "Look, kid, this isn't going to go well for you. Let's just get out of here. I'll buy you breakfast."

"I've killed people," the boy whispered.

The words took a moment to sink in. But Alex continued.

"I could just kill you. Get out."

Andrew was amazed that his voice didn't shake. "You're not going to kill me. You don't even want to. Breakfast. Come on."

"They want to," Alex said. His voice rose a little and cracked. "I can't stop them."

Andrew wanted to ask who "they" were.

But he knew he didn't really want to know.

Chris and Reese had been clear about this boy. He'd been possessed once—involved with something big.

Demons.

Something Andrew had no idea how to fight, and no ability to do so even if he were smart enough to know how.

Something that, judging from Alex's words, just might want that fight to happen.

But Alex himself was just standing there, a black-garbed statue, a teenage boy who looked like he was too scared—of his situation, of Andrew, of who knew what—to move.

And Andrew saw himself in the boy. A man frozen by things too big for him. Out of control, scared, and at the mercy of forces he could not see and had no idea how to handle.

He reached out. "Come on, Alex. Nobody's going to die right now. We can just get out of here together and grab something to eat and talk. Okay?"

Alex kept staring, his eyes growing larger. Moonlight picked up his eyes so they stood out, aglow, the most vivid thing in the shadowed room.

Andrew cleared his throat. "Come on."

A clock started to chime, and the sound broke whatever was holding Alex to the floor. He jumped like a scared rabbit and cursed too loudly.

A floor creaked overhead. Then footsteps, and a light came on. A man's voice, gruff and meaning business, called down the stairs: "Who's there?"

Andrew dropped to the ground, adrenaline surging, seconds before Alex all but threw himself out the window after him. Lights were coming on all over the house as the two bolted for the street. Andrew instinctively raced for the shadows of the house across the street.

But they'd left the window open. The owner would know what direction to look. They had to get out of sight.

Of course, chances were the guy would also wake the neighourhood.

He collared Alex in one swift move and hauled him to the left. They couldn't just run; someone would see them. Every house on the block would wake up once the would-be victim sounded the alarm. They needed a destination where they could actually get out of sight.

"This way," Andrew said through gritted teeth as he pulled Alex by the shirt collar after him. "My house."

Inwardly, he cursed the boy for dressing like a classic thief. If it were just him, he could pretend he was just out jogging and had happened to come across this street as the break-in was in progress. He could even say he'd seen the thief, running in some other direction. But not with Alex looking like this. He had guilt woven into every stitch of his clothing.

He didn't really know how fast they were going or how long it took them to round the corner, run up the next block, and reach the home stretch. Sirens sounded just as they reached his front door. Andrew threw the door open and tossed the kid inside, following him and locking up quick.

"Andrew, what—" Julie stopped midsentence when she recognized Alex. She looked at Andrew.

"I'll explain later. We should hide him." As an afterthought, he added, "He didn't do anything. Exactly."

Alex seemed too stunned, or too incapable, even to say anything. "In the garage," Andrew heard himself saying. "He can hide in the truck. They won't look—"

"Andrew," Julie said. She laid a calming hand on his shoulder, and the effect was almost instant. He shut his mouth and let that touch fill him.

"Is anyone after you?" she asked.

He worked his mind back, trying to recall their frantic flight in greater detail. Had he heard pursuit? Shouts? Any sign that anyone had seen them?

No.

Against his expectations, he hadn't heard the victim's voice again—the neighourhood hadn't come to life. There had been sirens, but they were already far away by the time those started to sound.

"No one's after us," he said. "But we might have been seen. It's not too early for people to be up for work; somebody could have seen us running."

"What happened?"

"Kid broke into a house. I saw him, recognized him, and tried to convince him to come with me."

"For breakfast," Alex put in.

They were the first two words he'd said, and they were so unexpected that Andrew had to grin. "Yeah, for breakfast. If you wanted it, you should have said yes sooner."

The sirens were quiet; Julie cracked the front door open, but no sounds came in from outside. The suburban street seemed to be mostly still sleeping in the cold. She raised an eyebrow in Andrew's direction.

"It's okay," he said. "Shut it. I don't think hiding in the truck is going to be necessary."

Alex's eyes darted from Julie to Andrew and back again. He was doing that stare thing again, and this time it got Andrew's back up. He didn't like the way the boy was looking at his wife.

"Hey," he said, giving Alex a smack to the back of the head. "Come upstairs, I'll give you something else to wear in case the cops come calling."

Alex got up out of the kitchen chair where he had collapsed after their run, body language grudging. He tore his eyes away from Julie. "Thanks."

"You're welcome," Andrew said. "If you're really grateful, you'll thank me by staying out of trouble." He motioned for Alex to precede him out of the kitchen and up the stairs, preferring to keep the boy in his sight. "What were you thinking, anyway?"

"I need money," the kid mumbled.

"And you can't get a job?"

"Never had one."

"It's easier than breaking into a house. Trust me."

He didn't want to admit it, but the boy's words shook him a little. The kid was what, seventeen? Eighteen? And he thought it was a good idea to stage a break-in rather than apply at some hamburger joint? Why?

Never mind all that demonic business. That was another side of the story altogether. It seemed to him that someone had failed this boy badly.

"It's not that hard," he continued as they trudged up the stairs. His legs were burning from the impromptu dash home. "You drop off a resume that says you're in high school, show up for work on time, flip a few burgers, get paid."

"I need more money than that."

"Uh-huh," Andrew said. "Like how much?"

"None of your business."

"What do you need it for?" He halted outside of his bedroom and opened the door. "In. You can pick out what you want to wear. I'm twenty years older than you but at least my clothes aren't all black."

Alex nodded and started slowly piecing through Andrew's closet, grabbing a pair of jeans and a button-up plaid shirt that was going to be way too big. Andrew's brain was still working on the job thing.

"You are in high school, right? Isn't that where you met Miranda?"

"I go sometimes," Alex mumbled.

He didn't sound happy about it. Andrew felt himself moving into lecture gear and wondered if he should hold back.

He decided not to.

"I don't think I have to tell you you're making bad choices. It doesn't have to be like this. You can finish school, get a real job. Whatever trouble you're in, you can get out. I'll help . . ."

"You don't know what you're talking about," Alex snapped. He held up the pile of clothes he'd picked. "Thanks for your help, but you don't know my life or anything about it. Shut the door, would you? I want to get dressed."

Andrew did, and waited impatiently in the hallway. He wanted to keep lecturing. Maybe it was all his concerns and fears for Miranda piling up in his mouth and spilling out at Alex. After all, the kid changing in his room was the friend his daughter had chosen. This punk who'd never had a job and only went to school "sometimes" and messed around with powers of darkness that were way bigger than any of them—that was the peer Miranda had decided to trust.

Great, Andrew thought. We may be in bigger trouble than I thought. Thank God April had managed to get through to Miranda to the extent that she did.

And yet, he wasn't really mad at Alex. Concerned for him, yes. He felt downright fatherly, in fact. By the time the door opened and Alex stood there looking awkward in clothes that were too big but made him look like a new person nonetheless, Andrew had decided that whatever trouble this boy was in, he was going to help him out of it.

And then he was going to help Alex get his feet on a new path in life. A good path. And maybe they could help Miranda some more in the process.

"Alex?" Miranda's voice drew both their attention. She was standing at the end of a hallway in a pink bathrobe, looking very surprised.

"Hey," Alex said.

"What are you doing here?"

"Your dad's helping me out," Alex said.

Andrew was surprised, and pleased, at the admission. "That's right," he said, "I am. Why don't you come downstairs and have breakfast?" he asked Alex. "Unless you still want to go out."

"No, that's okay. I can eat here."

Andrew narrowed his eyes and tried to parse the silent inter-action between his daughter and this kid; he didn't think he saw interest on Alex's end. And Miranda seemed more surprised and standoffish than anything else. This was just one more thing in a long line of things to process. She didn't say anything more to either of them, but she fell in line behind them as Andrew led the way to the kitchen. Julie was already getting breakfast ready. She turned and smiled as they entered.

But then there was Alex's reaction again—the same star-ing, the same stiffness. She turned away quickly, and Andrew frowned.

Alex wasn't just reacting to Julie.

Something in him was reacting to something in her.

In all the panic and attempt to escape the police, he had almost forgotten the boy's voice and threat in the house: "I could kill you." He had almost forgotten that Alex wasn't a little kid in trouble; he was actually dangerous.

He could see that now. But somehow it just made him even more determined to help. He stiffened his jaw and started coffee.

"Sit," he ordered, jarring Alex out of his stare. The teen dropped into a chair at the table and waited uncomfortably for food.

Julie set a plate of eggs and toast in front of him. Andrew watched out of the corner of his eye. She seemed as ill at ease as Alex was, and after delivering the plate she backed away from the table almost immediately. A moment later she laid her hand on Andrew's arm.

"Can I talk to you for a minute?" she asked.

"Sure," he said, his eye still half on Alex—and Miranda, who had decided to sit across the table from him.

They slipped into the living room, Andrew making sure he was still in Alex's eyesight.

"He's a mess," Julie said.

"You don't have to tell me that. He needs a family."

"Ye-es," she said, watching the teens at the table. Then she started. "Not our family?"

Andrew folded his arms. "He needs someone. We're as good as anyone."

"Have you seen . . . well, the way he . . ."

"Reacts to you?"

"Yes."

"That's a spirit thing."

"Yes," Julie said. "It is. Andrew, that kid is not any more alone than I am."

"I kind of thought so."

"We're not going to be able to help him while that's still the case."

"What are you saying?"

"That's a demon," Julie said bluntly. "He's possessed. You're not going to be able to help him unless you can get him free of that thing."

Andrew shook his head. "I thought Chris and Reese kicked something out of him when they found him at the corner store."

"They did, but maybe they didn't get everything. Or else the other one came back."

"They can come back?"

"Yes," Julie said. She looked troubled. "Demons don't give up real estate once they've got it."

"So what? Are you saying we can't help him?"

"There's one way," Julie said.

Andrew sighed. "Tell me."

"He has to become Oneness. If he does that, the Spirit will take possession of him, and the demons can't come back. That's the only way."

"But we can't make that happen."

"No."

"And I don't even know if I want that to happen."

"I know." Her blue eyes regarded him without pleading or anger. "I understand, Andrew. But the Oneness is the greatest good. It's not something to protect people from. Or to fight against."

"Are you telling me I'm fighting it?"

She smiled at that. "You tell me."

He didn't answer, and she shook her head. "I'm just scared,

Andrew. This is too much for you. If you try to help him some other way . . ."

"How about we cross bridges when we come to them? Can we do that?"

She nodded, but she didn't look happy.

"Shelley's coming again," Mary said in a worried tone of voice. "She wants to take Nick for a few days."

"Again?" April asked, pausing as she drew a mug out of the cupboard.

"Again. Three days this time."

"You don't like that."

"No," Mary admitted, "I don't. I know she's his mother, and there's nothing we can do about it—he's only living here because she lets him."

"Is his father around again?"

"Yes."

April poured a cup of coffee and looked worriedly into it as she stirred in cream and too much sugar. "Did he tell you much about how the last few times went?"

"No. Which is partly why I don't like this."

Since Shelley's first day visit, she'd been back to take Nick twice—the second time for a week.

Nick's picture of the fire in the living room, initialed and still awaiting a frame, still hung on the refrigerator. April smiled as she took it off. "I'll get him a frame today—have it waiting for him when he gets home. He'll like that."

Mary regarded her curiously. "Are you still drawing flame pictures of your own?"

"Not so much. I think I need to find other ways to understand it."

"And what ways are you trying?"

"Listening," April said. "And . . . well, that's about it, really. This fire is the Spirit, and the Spirit speaks. I'm trying to get better at listening for his voice."

Mary reached out and took April's hand, and they simply stood together for a few minutes, like mother and daughter— giving to each other, receiving from each other. When she let go and April's hand dropped back to her side, each woman had been warmed and strengthened by the other.

"I can feel the difference in you," Mary said. "It's almost frightening—and yet not. Something about it feels familiar. Like a call I've always meant to answer and never quite have."

"I don't know why me," April said.

"You're a great saint . . ."

"But why? Why isn't it you? Or Richard? You've both traveled this road so much longer than I have. And you can't tell me I'm greater than you are. You are certainly more faithful."

"I don't know why the Spirit operates the way he does," Mary said. "But I'm beginning to think we should ask more often, and maybe not stop asking until we get the answers."

"Why do you say that?" April asked with a smile.

"You told me, the other night, that you were beginning to realize the Spirit was a person. Remember? And then there's what Melissa said about love. Well, when I love someone, I want them to understand me. And if I'm hard to understand, I want them to try."

"I think all the Oneness feel that way." April paused. "Probably everyone does."

"But we feel it more—the hunger to be united. To be known as deeply as we can be known. Yes. If we feel that way because of the Spirit in us, and if he is also a person, then how does he feel? Does he want us to know him as deeply as he can be known?"

April thought about it. "The answer has to be yes."

"So," Mary said, "I think we should ask, and keep on asking, when we don't understand what he is doing."

"He has reasons," April said.

"I assume so. Does this life feel arbitrary to you?"

April laughed at that. "Anything but."

"Then we should let that be a lesson to us," Mary said.

"You remember my painting on the cave walls."

"Of course! Who could forget that?"

"They predicted things. Even some things we don't understand yet. I remember painting fire . . . but I didn't know what was coming. And the pictures explained other things. Like

Reese's story. And David. All of that came through the Spirit."

"So what does that tell you?" Mary asked, leaning against the kitchen counter.

"That you're right. Nothing is arbitrary. And there are reasons . . . answers, if we'll ask for them."

April thought a moment. "Maybe we need to get better at asking the right questions too." Like who we are. And who the Spirit is. And what death and life really mean. It suddenly seemed incredible to her that they could have been fighting their battles all these years without ever really understanding those things.

She glanced at the clock. "When is Shelley coming?"

"In about an hour. Nick's upstairs, 'getting ready.'"

April thought she knew what that looked like. As a kid when she had to be with someone who didn't feel safe, she would obsess over "organizing" her things—mostly packing and repacking and repacking the few meagre belongings she had, and adding anything extra she could find. Because it helped give her a sense of preparation and a tiny sense of control. At least, that's why she thought she had done it. She wondered if she should go upstairs and try to talk to Nick about the upcoming visit. Silently, in spirit, she reached out—yes, she could feel him up there, feel the frantic edge to whatever he was doing.

Sigh.

She fought back an urge to just take him somewhere for the day, conveniently disappear. They couldn't do that to his mother. Right? Anyway, they didn't need her calling the police on them. The Oneness's relationship with Shelley had grown distinctly rockier since her initial rush of gratitude for their getting Nick away from the hive. For a time they had hoped she might come into the Oneness herself, but instead she had gravitated back to her old life, and the more she drank and spent time with Nick's father, the less she liked or trusted the cell. On one occasion when she felt they were overstepping their boundaries, she had threatened to call the cops. And their relationship with the police was, likewise, rockier than formerly. There was the whole cemetery thing, and the fact that Reese had failed to bring back their star prisoner and instead apparently lost him to death.

No, it was probably best that they not "lose" anyone else, even just temporarily in an attempt to get a boy away from parents who were the most unstable and damaging thing in his life.

At least she could try to calm him down.

She headed upstairs and knocked on his door, listening to the hasty shuffle on the other side.

"Yeah?"

"It's me, Nick. Let me in."

He opened the door and poked a blond head out. "It's not locked."

"I try to respect your privacy."

"Thanks."

She peered past him. Clothes—most of them bought for him during an afternoon shopping trip with Richard and Mary, since the few things he'd brought with him were ratty and too cold for the coming winter—were strewn everywhere around an open duffel bag, along with most of Nick's other belongings.

"You're just going out for a couple of days," she commented.

"I'm taking stuff just in case."

"In case of what?" She eased onto the bed, pushing aside a mound of clothing and a few comic books. "What are you worried about?"

"I dunno, just in case."

"It's okay, Nick," April said. "It's okay for you to feel like this. But you'll be coming back here. We aren't going to lose you. Look, I'll make you a deal: fish and chips when you get back."

"At the pub?"

"Yes."

"Are you gonna buy me a new sketchbook?"

"Are you through with the old one?" April asked, surprised.

"Almost."

"Okay. I'll buy you a new one. But you have to try to draw something new. You're getting stuck in a rut with all these flames."

"I will if you will," he said, a twinkle in his eye. She laughed, glad to have moved his mind onto something else—onto something good in the future, something to look forward to and work toward. Something that would anchor him to his new life even when he was temporarily back in the old one.

It's just for a few days, she reminded herself. You're as bad as Nick, acting like he's going away for weeks or something.

But there was a very real sense of foreboding in the air. She wondered if she should pay attention to that.

No, she decided. She was just feeling the remnants of her own childhood. Nick brought so much of that back for her. But he also reminded her of how far she had come. That that life was long, long gone.

As it would be for him, eventually.

The Oneness was his life now, as it was hers.

She considered that she was going through another transition now. That the Spirit himself was becoming her new home and she was leaving an old life behind again. That thought, springing out of nowhere, left her feeling a little shaken. She loved this life. She wasn't sure she was ready to leave it.

Or that she trusted where she was going.

She chided herself silently. You're not leaving anything behind. The Oneness is still home. The Oneness is part of the Spirit, remember?

The moment of connection with Mary in the kitchen just minutes ago reassured her now.

Nick seemed happier after her promise of a new sketchbook, and she noticed that he didn't stuff everything he had laying out into the duffel bag—though he still packed enough for a week away at least, including comic books. She looked around and tossed a packet of pencil crayons his direction.

"Here, catch."

He did. "What?"

"Pack those."

"Why?"

"Because if you get free time, you should draw comic books, not just read 'em. You're an artist. Daily discipline, remember?"

"Fine," he said, stuffing them into the bag. She smiled. One more link with home—the charge from her, a commitment to keep, a more significant tie even than her promise.

"You got paper?"

"Yeah," he said.

"Good. Work on something good for me, if you get a few minutes."

"I am," Nick said proudly. "I'm working on a comic book about Richard."

"Richard?"

"Yeah, and the hive wars."

She hid a smile. "I like it."

And she did.

Nick's face had figured large in her painting in the cave. She didn't know why, but he had a bigger part in this story than any of them knew yet. So it seemed right that in his eleven-year-old way, he was chronicling it. And he couldn't have chosen a better hero.

*   *   *   *   *

The day they began to bring all of the dying aboveground dawned clear and crisp, the chill burning off as the sun rose higher. The guards had been conscripted for the task of carrying litters of diseased men and women and children up the narrow stairways of the castle, into the sun, and then under the shelter of the tents that had turned the courtyard into a veritable town. Most tents were open to the air, entire sides pulled back.

Teresa oversaw the work until she was satisfied they were being handled with proper care; then she disappeared into the chapel and reappeared carrying the first finished painting. She had worked on it long into the night, disdaining to return to her quarters until the early hours of morning—even then, if she hadn't known sleep was necessary to service on this day, she might have remained in the chapel until sunrise.

Ten years ago, the paintings had simply been placed wherever the most eyes could see them. That was harder here, with the sick divided into tents, so she picked up her easel and the painted wooden panel and set it in the centre of the largest tent, where eight different pallets lay with their occupants in various stages of wasting away.

She did not remember, ten years ago, that placing her work within the sight of the diseased made any immediate difference.

But it did now.

Perhaps she was simply more sensitive to it this time—but she saw it in their eyes, in their mouths, in the tone of their skin. It was as though sunlight was shining directly on them, and it changed their aspect entirely. So much so that she caught her breath when she turned away from setting the painting up and took in their faces.

And then there was Tildy, who had come in sometime while the painting was being set up, and was staring at it now with her jaw slack and her entire posture frozen in place—

Seeing herself, maybe truly, for the first time.

Teresa hadn't realized until this moment how much power there could be in that.

She crossed the tent floor to Tildy's side. The girl looked at her bewildered, and Teresa drew her under her wing and said, "I asked the Spirit for a picture, and that is what he drew through me. Can you see how beautiful it is?"

She nodded dumbly, and then tore her eyes away, looking around at the sick while she dashed tears from her narrow face. That they could see the beauty too was clear—there was still, on their countenances, that sense that the sun was shining.

Tildy returned her attention to an ailing woman as some of the less-helpful of the servants arrived, carrying buckets of water and gruel. She kept her expression downcast, and Teresa saw fear and shame in the way she moved—as though she did not want any of her fellows to know that for a moment, she had seen herself as something radiant.

But the sick themselves had no such fears. Murmurs rose, and then gasps, and Teresa watched in amazement as some began to push themselves up on their pallets, rising for a clearer view.

And then one, a child of thirteen or fourteen summers who had been near death only the night before, was on her feet—standing fascinated before the painting, tracing Tildy's face with a finger.

It took a moment for everyone to truly realize what was happening. In fact, it was one of the surlier servants who voiced it first.

"Impossible," he said. "The girl is healed!"

Things then began to happen very fast. Teresa turned to see Tildy helping the woman she had been tending to her feet, and across the tent, a man was trying his own legs. Nor did they let him down. Murmurs turned to shouts, and then to laughter, and she heard the words whispering and then rioting through the air—"A miracle! A miracle! They are healed! A miracle!"

Franz Bertoller, drawn by the shouts, stood in the entrance of the tent with surprise and something else lighting his face—something she could not identify but remembered. That expression had been there ten years ago.

Confusion.

Back then, she had seen enmity in it.

Now, she didn't know what to think it was.

Two of the servants were wrestling the painting of Tildy off its easel, shouting something about taking it to another tent. To more of the dying. Teresa thought she should intervene but didn't know how, or why—she didn't really know what was happening.

This was far, far out of her control.

Tildy appeared at her elbow and tugged at her. "Come," she said, breathless, "come with us to see if the miracle will spread." The men carrying the painting seemed unsteady on their feet, and suddenly it looked as though they would all go down—they staggered, not from the weight of the thin panel, but as though they were drunk. "Be careful with that!" Tildy shouted after them, still tugging insistently at Teresa.

Shaking her head, Teresa gave in and followed the growing crowd to the next tent. She found as she walked that the ground seemed to tip under her—as though something in the air inebriated them all. Sounds of laughter joined the shouts, and beside her one of the servants fell to his knees and began to laugh uproariously, holding his ribs, tears running down his face.

"What is this?" Teresa asked the air. Her next step lurched, and her legs would not hold her up; she bent slowly to her knees—and something drew her eyes up.

The courtyard was full of golden light, as from a great fire burning in the day. On all sides, men and women were on their knees and hands and faces on the courtyard stones, some crying, some laughing, many shouting. More and more of the diseased were emerging from tents—many had not even seen the painting yet, but the miracle worked of its own accord. But it was none of that that riveted Teresa's attention.

It was the vision of a figure like a man standing in the air above the courtyard holding a sword in one hand and a wineskin in the other. Light poured forth as wine from the skin, flowing through the air into the courtyard. The figure was tall, golden, and shining so brightly that his features were obscured.

And yet, Teresa knew when his eyes turned to her, and her breath escaped her lungs when the great shining head nodded at her—as one who acknowledges a friend.

And then the eyes were raised and fixed on one who stood at the back of the courtyard, on the steps of the castle. Teresa turned her head and followed the gaze as it fastened on their host, the lord of the castle, with his expression that had turned to fear.

Though his eyes did not indicate that he could see the figure standing in the midst of the hilarity of healing, Franz turned abruptly and disappeared into the castle, slamming the door behind him.

* * * * *

Shelley was due to bring Nick back after three days. April spent the three days trying not to think about him too much. Now and again she tried to reach out through the Oneness and sense how he was doing, but he was far away, and the connection wasn't strong enough. That was probably a good sign—she thought she would know if he was in any serious distress.

But her own memories of home visits kept her from relaxing fully until he was back home in the cell house.

She talked Richard into agreeing that she could take Nick out for the promised pub food as soon as he got home. He was supposed to get back at four o'clock on Sunday afternoon, and given Shelley's track record, April figured they would be about an hour late.

By five-thirty, she had stopped perching on the counter and taken to pacing the kitchen; by six, she was openly worried and alternating between checking the clock, looking out past the lace curtains to see if anyone had driven up without her hearing them, and trying to reach out in the Spirit for some sense of where Nick was and what was happening to him.

"It's okay, April," Richard said, sitting at the kitchen with a book and his reading glasses. "Shelley's late. She's always late."

"I don't know," April said, rubbing her arms. "I just don't . . ."

She didn't know why she stopped. Nothing happened to cut her off; she heard nothing, saw nothing. But she had a sudden sense of needing to pay attention.

And when she did, she felt something through the Oneness. A shift.

He wasn't okay.

She grabbed her coat from the hook near the door. "Something's wrong. I'm going to find him."

"Where?" Richard asked, taking off his glasses and standing. "Where are you going to look?"

"I don't know. I just need to find him. He's not okay; I can feel it."

"You can't just rush out there, April. We need something to go on."

The "we" was reassuring, and Richard was right—April stopped with the door half-open, letting in an icy wind, and thought a moment. "Shelley's house. Maybe they're just over there."

Richard was already grabbing his hat and keys. Even through her growing anxiety, April thought of Nick's comic book and smiled. His hero was coming to rescue him. No trace of the fear she had felt toward Richard only a short time ago was left—she wasn't sure how she had ever compared him to her father, even for a moment.

Maybe when you were trying hard not to open yourself up to the Spirit or to let it—him—act in a way that was outside of your control, it shut you off from the truth of other people too.

In any case, there was no one she would rather have with her now.

The air outside the door was biting cold and winter dark, offset by the moon on the bay below and the glow of striped remnants of a recent light snowfall. April could see her breath in the light over the front door. She rubbed her hands together as Richard started his car and drove it up so she could jump in. The engine strained against the cold as they coasted down the road and turned toward the lower-income area where Nick had lived the last several years. Always awake at night, the neighbourhood was darkened by drawn shades and doors and porches sealed shut against the cold. In the summer, the street was awake to the blare of TVs, the bark of dogs, and the shouts of people—mothers yelling at their kids, kids yelling at their dogs, men yelling at each other. In comparison, the street in winter was eerily silent.

Richard's headlights swept up a road marked with potholes and blowing trash from a metal can that had tipped over and not been righted. The can itself rolled in the gutter on the side of the street.

He pulled into a driveway.

"This is it."

April stared through the dark. "No, it's not. It was more . . ."

"This is it," Richard said. "It's the right address."

She didn't want to say it, and he didn't either. Not only did it not look like anyone was there, but it didn't look like any had been there recently—

Maybe not in months.

April got out and drew a deep breath before she knocked on the front door. Not anticipating an answer, she stalked across the yard and tried to peer through the dark front window. Nothing. No one.

Richard was at the front door now, so she kept going, circling around the side, past a couple of trash cans—empty and chained to the wall—to a chain-link gate that led to a tiny yard in the back. The chain hung loose, so she pushed it open and crept into the shadows behind the house. There was no sign of inhabitants back here either. Her feet crunched on snow, and she banged on the back window just in case.

"April," Richard's voice came from around the side, "we should go. No one's here."

She wanted to argue, but he was right.

Worse, when she tried to reach out for Nick, she could still feel distress—but she had no idea how to find him.

Voices on the other side of the house grabbed her attention—Richard talking to someone who sounded agitated. She came around to the front, into the headlight beams, and shielded her eyes to see Richard talking to a woman in a ratty coat. He waved for her to get into the car, so she did, and waited. He joined her after a few minutes.

"What was that about?" April asked.

"The landlady. Thought we were a couple of burglars. She lives across the street."

"Does she know where they are?"

In the dim light, April could make out concern on Richard's face. "Not here."

"We could see that for ourselves."

"It's worse than that," Richard said. "April, she says they haven't lived here in two months."

"What?"

"Shelley was behind on her rent; the landlady evicted her. She doesn't know where she went. Says she hasn't seen her around here since."

"Why didn't Nick tell us?" April said. "On his last visits . . . he made it sound like they came here."

"Apparently not."

Her breath was starting to come a little faster.

"It's okay," Richard said.

"No, it's not. He's practically been lying to us; that's a bad sign, Richard. And you should have seen him before this visit . . . and I can still feel him. He's in trouble. Where . . ."

"Can you tell where he is?"

"Of course I can't!" The words burst out of her. "You know it doesn't work like that!"

"I'm not sure we know how 'it' works as well as we think we do. I just thought I'd ask."

His hand was on her shoulder—she didn't know when he'd put it there. Panic rose in her, and for once it wasn't accompanied by the heat in her soul—and for once, she wished it was. That heat was power, and right now, she needed power.

"Come on," she said under her breath. "Come on, come on, come on . . ."

"April, it's all right. We'll find him." She heard the words he wasn't actually saying: Calm down. You need to calm down.

Why? Was he afraid of her? Afraid of the heat, of the fire?

But it wasn't going to burn. It wasn't there. Wasn't there now that she needed it most, now that she wasn't afraid of it. Or at least, now that her need outweighed her fear.

"Okay, think, Richard," Richard said. Talking out loud at least as much to calm her down as to keep himself focused, but she appreciated it even though she saw through the action. "How do we find them? She's been living somewhere—so we check rentals and find out if she rented somewhere else. Only places that would be willing to rent to someone with bad credit."

"Or she's staying with someone else," April said. "Maybe her ex."

"Husband?" Richard asked.

"That's who I meant," April said, her stomach sinking. But the question brought up the possibility that Shelley had just moved in with some other boyfriend, past or present. And who knew where that might be.

"I can start calling around from the office first thing in the morning," Richard said.

"I don't want to wait that long."

"Neither do I. But I'm not going to reach anyone tonight."

April closed her eyes, her hands braced on the dashboard. She reached out, trying to find him—encountering the sense of distress once again, a sense shrouded in fear. Whether Nick was afraid or she was just feeling her own fear in response to him, she didn't know, but she couldn't calm herself down any more than she already had. This all felt too raw. Too personal.

Too much like she herself was in trouble, with all of her nerves open and expecting a battering.

And then, small and fainter than a whisper, came a question: Where would you be?

And the answer was easy.

Running.

If she were in Nick's shoes, she would be running.

And if he was in this town, she knew where he would go. She doubted he could find his way up to the cell house in the dark—too many unfamiliar streets between their neighbourhood and wherever he was. But he could run toward the bay. All he had to do was follow the sloping streets straight down.

And if he got there, she thought she knew where he would go.

"The pub," she said. "Can we go to the pub? I think he's running. I think he'll go there."

Richard was already backing into the street. "On our way."

The lights on the streets increased as they got closer to the harbour. April counted as they drove, letting the numbers keep her focused, and her eyes searched the streets for a small, skinny form pelting toward the bay—running, like she'd seen him do so many times before. Before he was one of theirs. Before she cared so much about him that she could taste his need now, like a bitterness constricting her throat. She wanted him to be sitting beside her, pestering her with questions about drawing and Oneness and fires.

Oh, fires.

They were on the street that ran along the wharf, and Richard slowed down so they could scan the streets and shadows more thoroughly. There wasn't much traffic down here at this hour—most of the businesses were still open, but only a handful of patrons were abroad.

Richard pulled up in front of the pub, and April jumped out of the car and pushed through the front door into the noisy glow of the place. Nick wouldn't be allowed inside at this hour, especially not on his own, but he was a decent hand at sneaking in.

No sign of him.

But his dad was there.

April had run into Nick's father once or twice in the days before he came and joined them at the cell house. It had always been here, sitting at that bar, where he'd usually had too much to drink. He wasn't a big man, or an especially mean one, but his relationship with Shelley was rocky enough to make for a volatile life together.

April pushed her way up to him at the bar and asked without preamble, "Do you know where Nick is?"

"What?" he asked, his eyes opening wide in surprise and then narrowing at her. "I remember you. You're that . . ."

"Please, I just need to know—have you seen Nick?"

"Ain't you his guardian now? Doesn't he live with you?"

"He does, but he was visiting his mother."

He thumped a half-empty stein on the bar. 'And you expect me to know where he is? Ain't seen her in months. She replaced me with some good-for-nothing—"

"Who?" April asked. "Do you know his name? Or where he lives?" She forced herself to sound calmer. "Shelley didn't bring Nick back to me, and I'm . . . concerned about him. I'm trying to find out where he might be."

Nick's dad—Toby, she remembered—leaned back and regarded her skeptically for what seemed like an eternity. His seat on the barstool looked a little unsteady, and she silently prayed that he wasn't too drunk to know what she was asking.

Finally he said, "Guy's name is Sanders. Tom Sanders."

"Does he live here in town?"

"No, up the coast a ways. Takes a couple of days to get there. He's a fisherman. Works up and down the bay."

April's heart sank even farther. A couple of days? Why hadn't Nick told them Shelley was taking him so far? Assuming, of course, that she had taken him there before and that she hadn't held visitation in some more local halfway place.

"Is Shelley living with him?" she asked.

"For the last three months. Don't ask me why. I tried to be good to her. Woman can't be pleased."

"And Nick?" April asked, her voice shaking slightly. "You think he's safe with them?"

"He's a tough kid." But Toby's eyes betrayed some worry. "He's been through more than he should, probably. I don't know Sanders, if he's violent or not. Shelley always had bad taste in men."

Nodding, at the irony of the comment and in recognition that Toby had told her all he could, April pulled away. "Thank you."

"You going to find my kid?"

She gave him a grim smile. "We're going to try."

The day after the wave of miracle healing, several of the villagers fell ill again. It didn't take long before the disease reestablished its hold. Some of the healed had gone home; Teresa hoped they were still well. In any case, they never reappeared at the castle. But of those who had stayed, more than half were stricken again, and the servants were soon back to their unhappy service. The painting of Tildy remained in the courtyard, and some of the sick agitated to be positioned where they could see it, but it was as though the power was gone. Franz Bertoller, grim and stolid, said nothing to Teresa either about the healings or about the subsequent relapse.

Teresa herself alternated between resignation and feeling crushed.

She didn't know what had happened the day before—other than that it had manifested the Spirit, his glory, his personhood. She had seen him. And she would never forget the sight. But the miracle had not been under her control, and neither was this reappearance of disease under her control. She was helpless. And hated that fact.

Caring for the sick on that first day after the miracle was no easier than it had been before. As some of the victims cursed and wept bitter tears, even so caring for them was bitter.

Teresa worked that day till she thought her back would break, and in the end refused to go back to her quarters. She simply could not. Instead, she retired to the chapel, lit candles, and knelt to pray all night.

This time, with the image of a bright man in her mind's eye, holding sword and wineskin.

Teresa had long ago learned to function on only a few hours of sleep; her spirit was stronger than her flesh, and if she was troubled in spirit, or wanted to seek after the Spirit who sustained hers, sleep would elude her. Her body ached with exhaustion as she dropped to her knees, but she knew she would not doze, even in the soft light of the candles. She lit incense and let its fragrance rise, beckoning her soul to join it.

She did not anticipate the vision, but it came. And changed everything in an instant.

* * * * *

Tildy met Teresa in the castle corridor as she hurried over the flagstones in the early morning intent on confronting Franz Bertoller. The girl looked worried, and she reached out to clutch Teresa's arms as she spoke.

"Where are you rushing to, my lady?"

Teresa hardly looked at her. "I must speak with the lord."

"But . . . now? Have you eaten?"

Teresa forced herself to focus on the girl in front of her. "Tildy, it's all right. I have to speak to the lord. I can eat later. I'm all right."

But the fear didn't vanish from Tildy's face even a little. She was white, and Teresa could see that she was shaking.

"Please, my lady," she said, her voice strained, "it's not . . . you shouldn't . . ."

"Don't be afraid," Teresa said softly. Fixing her eyes on the girl's face, she gently removed her arms from Tildy's clutches and took her hands, assuring her that she would not rush away. "What is it?"

"I shouldn't trust the lord," Tildy blurted out. "You mustn't . . . he . . ."

"Not here," Teresa said, looking up and down the corridor. "Come with me, Tildy. Come and tell me what you want to tell me. What you've wanted to tell me all this time."

The girl had tears in her eyes, but she nodded. Hand in hand, Teresa led her back out of the castle and to the chapel. Tildy crossed the threshold with a visible abundance of nerves, her eyes darting around the tiny place of worship. They fixed on the altar, and Teresa saw her go pale again.

"What is it?" she asked.

Tildy pointed to the cloth over the altar. "He died there," she said woodenly.

"What? Who?"

"Can't you see the bloodstains?" Tildy asked. "The old priest. The lord killed him there."

Teresa felt the blood drain from her own face. She had noticed the stains—but she'd seen them as mud, as neglect, not as what they were.

"The lord killed the priest here, and he poisoned his own father on the same day," Tildy said. "I remember the day, though I were only a small bairn."

"I had no idea," Teresa said.

But she knew something else. She wondered if Tildy shared this terrible knowledge too. The knowledge that she had been rushing to confront the lord over—the knowledge given to her in vision.

All this time, as drawn as she was to the Oneness and the Spirit, Tildy had resisted being Joined. She had always been afraid. And for the first time, Teresa understood why.

"Do you know?" Teresa asked quietly. "Do you know what else he is guilty of?"

"Aye, he killed all the Oneness," Tildy said. "There were many in his father's day. He hunted them down and killed them all."

Teresa looked down, her stomach lurching.

She hadn't known that.

"He only left this chapel standing to remind us," Tildy said. "He threatens all with death who would become One. So you must forgive me for resisting you . . . I . . ."

"Forgive you!" Teresa cried. "Oh, Tildy, there is nothing

to forgive. But you must not allow fear to keep you from the Spirit. The Spirit is life. Fear is death. Now that you know all these things, now that you have seen the power of the Spirit, you must reject fear and choose life."

Tildy simply stared at her with wide, fearful eyes. "All the sick," the servant girl said. "They are those who joined with him in his persecution of the Oneness, and their families. He made a covenant with them to destroy the Oneness and keep them out of our land. I do not understand why he brought you here."

Why indeed?

"Then he has betrayed them," Teresa said, deciding that Tildy did not know what the Spirit had shown her in the dark of the night. "For the disease is of his own making. As it was ten years ago, in my country. He has conjured it through his own dark power, through his alliance with demons. That is why it has returned. Because he took up arms against the Spirit and recalled the disease to this place."

Tildy hugged herself, thin arms wrapped around thin body. "It is a great evil," she said, wonderingly. "Can any power be so great?"

"You can answer that yourself," Teresa said. "You saw the miracles yesterday. You have seen the Spirit in me. Is the power of darkness greater than what you have seen?"

"I do not think so," Tildy whispered. "But is the Spirit not losing now?"

"No," Teresa said. "Did you see him yesterday?"

"See the Spirit?"

"Yes."

"I don't know what you mean."

"I did," Teresa said. "In a waking vision. I saw a man shining like the sun, with a sword in one hand and a wineskin in the other. The wineskin spoke of healing, joy, and life; it was the source of the laughter that swept across the castle grounds as the healing went forth. But the sword—the sword spoke of battle and judgment. I tell you this, Tildy, whatever may come, the Spirit will not lose. He cannot. No doubt Bertoller intended that all who were healed yesterday should come back under the power of disease; that did not happen. Many have returned to their homes and others are still well even here. Only some have succumbed again. And you tell me many of these were in covenant with him against the Spirit?"

"All," Tildy said. "They all."

"Then we should not be surprised if there is a sword against them. I thank you for telling me all these things," Teresa said. "And for warning me. But I must go to the lord and confront him for the evil he is doing. He cannot go unchallenged."

"But you . . . why must you challenge him? He is not your lord."

"But he fights against the power in me," Teresa said, "against the Spirit I serve. And many years ago he attacked my own power as he learned to wield disease like a sword. He brought death where I tried to bring healing. He cannot simply go on unchecked."

"But I am afraid he will kill you," Tildy said.

Teresa smiled, refusing to show the fear that she felt—the certainty that Tildy was right and the degree to which she did not feel ready to face death. The knowledge that her premonitions about the man had been so right—and far more so than she had imagined—was nearly crushing. She questioned now her own motives in coming here, the idealist hope that she could somehow change him. But now that she was here, now that she knew what she knew, she had to confront him. There was simply no question about that.

For the first time, she was glad Niccolo had not come. Better that he was not here for this.

Still smiling, strong in front of Tildy, she said, "He may kill me. But my spirit will live on in the Spirit. And light has come to this place, Tildy—I do not think the darkness will be allowed to reign unchallenged again. Others will rise up to challenge its sway."

She locked her gaze with Tildy's so the girl could not look away. "Others. You. Don't fight the Spirit, Tildy. Life itself is not worth more than he is. Until you have entered into his being, you are not alive. You must believe me."

"I know you are right," Tildy said. "I have felt it many times—that you are alive where we are only half so. The Spirit in you draws me, calls to me."

"Then answer that call."

"But he will kill all who do," she said, bewildered. "More blood will stain this altar."

"But not in vain," Teresa said. "Never in vain."

She turned, paused in the doorway of the chapel, and drew a deep breath that Tildy could not see or hear. She could not let her own fear show—not only because she did not want this girl on the verge of overcoming to see it, but because she knew that if she let it become visible, it would overcome her too.

She would run.

And she could not, would not, do that.

* * * * *

"Tom Sanders," April said, sliding into the car next to Richard. "Shelley's new boyfriend. Nick's dad was in there—he thinks they'll be with Tom Sanders."

"And that would be . . ."

"Up the coast somewhere. Several days' drive. He doesn't know more than that."

"Can you still feel him?" Richard asked.

"Yes."

"I'm sorry, April."

"For what?" She turned to regard her old friend. He looked drawn.

"That we didn't keep better track of him. For his sake, and for yours. We should have paid more attention to your concerns."

"Maybe," April said, sitting back against the leather seat. "I don't know. I worry too much. I just wish we knew where to find him."

"A name is a start. I can trace that. Maybe even tonight, if he's got a record or anything I can easily look up."

April closed her eyes. The thought of Sanders having a record didn't make her any happier. "Yeah." She grimaced. "I was so sure he'd be here. Wishful thinking, I guess."

Anger at Shelley rose up, sudden and violent, and she wished again for the fire of the Spirit burning in her. Why was it so dull? Why now? And how could Shelley do this—how could she be so selfish as to put her own son in danger, pulling him out of a happy home where he was safe and thriving for the first time in his life, all because she wanted the gratification of feeling like a mother—even if she was a terrible one?

Bile rose up in the back of her throat.

"Are you okay, April?" Richard asked.

"Yes. No. I don't know. This is all so close to home for me. I feel like it's me out there. Only it's worse, because I thought I could protect myself, and I don't think Nick can."

"Nick has something you didn't. He has the Spirit."

"I hope it does him good," April muttered. "I have the Spirit too, but it's not doing much for me at the moment."

Richard looked at her curiously, but he didn't say a word—just started driving. "I'm going to the office," he said. "To try to look up our friend Sanders. You coming, or you want me to drop you back at the house?"

"I'm coming," April said. She had no desire to go home now. Not without having found Nick. It would feel too much like failure, or like giving up.

But she grew angrier as they drove across the village to the legal office where Richard worked. Angrier, more lost, more unhappy. And she found as they drove that most of her anger was turning inward, to where the fire was supposed to be. To where the Spirit supposedly was, silent and inactive.

What kind of time is this to stop speaking? she asked. Why

show up all the time when I don't want you, and now that I do, drop me?

Hot tears stung at her eyes. She was a child again, a victim of a father's violence and a mother's neglect. Like fire and cold, heat and silence.

They pulled into the parking lot behind the office. Richard parked and then paused, his hands resting on the wheel, his head turned slightly in April's direction but his eyes not actually looking at her—nonconfrontational but clearly having something to say. She waited for him to say it.

"Don't be alone," he said finally.

"I can't help it," she snapped.

"You might not be able to hear right now, but that doesn't mean nobody's there. You've still got the Oneness. I know the things you've experienced have been isolating you somewhat, but that doesn't change what you are—what we are."

"I appreciate that," she said, although she found his words as annoying as reassuring.

She was the painter from the cave, the great saint who had encountered the Spirit in the womb of the world and set loose a fire of vengeance, deliverance, and power. She was one whose experiences no one else could understand or enter into, one who could bring a new kind of vision and life.

Did that mean she didn't need the Oneness?

Or that she thought she didn't?

Maybe Richard's words rankled because he was right, and he was calling her out—gently—for her pride.

As she got out of the car and followed Richard into the office building, she sent up a prayer into the cold, dark sky. Okay! I'm sorry! I surrender . . . whatever it is that I'm doing wrong. Just please, please help me.

Richard flicked the office lights on, and April just wanted to collapse in an office chair and cry. Her legs and arms and hands and feet were so cold, and she felt empty. Beyond herself. Exhausted.

Richard unlocked a couple of filing cabinets and fired up the office computer while April watched, dull and hurting at the same time. Thoughts of Nick plagued her like an ache in her stomach.

She just wanted him to be okay.

While Richard searched through files, he started to hum. The melody was low and rich, and she recognized it as one he had hummed for years—just to himself, half under his breath, a part of who he was.

She closed her eyes and let his baritone sink into her soul.

The sound of a life changed. Her life changed. The sound of security and peace after a childhood of fear, where a man's voice was always a frightening thing and music was always loud and blaring. The sound of slow years of healing and change, before the cave, before the hive, before the fire.

And there, curled up in a chair listening to Richard sing, she heard the Spirit again.

I was there, the still voice said. All those years. I was the song and the healer and the safety you knew.

But you scare me now, she said. I don't understand you.

Then hang on to what you already know. I am not changed. I am only more than you thought when you first knew me.

Part of her wanted to ask—since the voice was talking now—where Nick was. But part of her didn't. Part of her just wanted to sit here and listen to the Spirit and talk to him, because she realized that her anger had come from thinking she was abandoned.

And she had been wrong.

Anyway, although she couldn't explain why or how she knew this, she realized that whatever this person-to-person relationship with the Spirit was, it didn't guarantee getting answers. She wasn't just going to be able to ask any question and immediately learn what she wanted to know. Even if the answer felt important to her.

Right now, it was good just to know that she wasn't alone.

She sat and basked in that for a while, losing track of time. She snapped back into the real world when the office door opened to a mittened hand, and Mary walked in and took a seat beside her. Without a word, she reached over and gathered April's hand in her own.

Only seconds later, Melissa and Alicia came through the door, and Diane, Chris, and Reese after them. Tyler was a few minutes later, but he came too. No one really said anything. They all just took their seats around the office and joined hearts and waited for Richard to say something. He looked up and smiled at each one who entered, but he didn't say a word.

Half an hour later, Tony and Angelica spilled through the door and sat on the floor, the only space left, at Chris and Tyler's feet.

April didn't understand. She didn't know why they were here or how they had known to come—especially the twins, who must have driven in. But her heart wanted to burst.

With the reality, the power of not being alone.

She closed her eyes and let herself feel the truth of the Oneness. The more she let herself go into it, the more fully she felt it all: the heartbeats, pulses, breath in lungs. Souls intertwined. Thoughts and feelings winding around each other. They were all veins in the same stream, the same blood pulsing through all of them. One body, one heart, one Spirit: Oneness. All being sought and known and shaped by the same Worker in the womb in the world.

And they were all going to find Nick, and bring him home, together.

Niccolo reined his horse in at a watering trough in a cold village just south of Franz Bertoller's mountain city. According to the maps he'd been following, he was close. His heart told him the same. Teresa wasn't far. Mother to him, sister to him, muse and confidante to him, this one whom he loved was near.

If it hadn't been for the disease that knocked him off his feet for weeks after her departure, he would have been here long ago. But the battle had been harder fought than anyone expected, and demonic voices plagued his dreams—taunting him with threats and visions of failure and death.

Never had he had such an experience. The sisters had tended him with all their skill and compassion, but it was thoughts of Teresa that pulled him through. An unaccountable conviction that she needed him.

He had always counted himself in debt to Teresa. Without her not only would his life have ended in the miserable plague of his childhood, but he should never have come into the Oneness;

and not only would he never have known Oneness, but without her he would never have discovered his gifts, his remarkable art, the way he could help others, his place in the world.

He was not happy to find she had gone off without him, although it didn't surprise him—she had always been headstrong and determined. She complained when he followed her example in that, but they both knew where he had learned it.

Dismounting, he stretched his legs while his horse watered itself. The village was small and dirty; a chill in the air did little to mitigate the smell of refuse mingling with smoke from hearthfires and the forge of a nearby blacksmith. Eyes fixed on him; loiterers and tradesmen stared. He tried to ignore them. He had a bad habit of getting drawn into the lives of people he encountered, and right now, he didn't want to lose any more time finding Teresa. He shivered, not wanting to admit how much the cold and damp were affecting him. He'd thought he'd left the fever behind him, but eight days into his journey, it seemed to want to come back for a second bout. He was doing his best to deny its chances.

"Ho, stranger," a gruff voice greeted him.

He looked up to see a man of middling height and middling girth, with a bushy beard and sharp eyes, standing only a few feet away. The man was looking him over carefully, but there was no real threat in his manner.

"I am just passing through," Niccolo said. "My horse was thirsty, and I . . ."

"No need, no need," the man said. "You're welcome enough. I suspect you may be thirsty also, aye?"

Niccolo intended to say no, but the truth came out his

mouth instead. "In truth, it has been some days since I had much else but spring water."

"Then come in, and have a drink. I am the innkeeper here."

"It's good of you, but I fear I'm short on coin, and on time."

"The coin is not necessary; twas I who offered the drink, not you who tried to take it. As for time, your horse could use an hour's rest, and so from the looks of you could you. You can ride off again hastily if you please, but I wager you'll soon be slowed by exhaustion. Come, boy, take my advice and rest a little while."

Niccolo opened his mouth to protest, but the man's good sense overcame his protests before he had time to form them. He found himself nodding instead, and tying his horse to the post.

"I thank you," he said. "I think my journey must not be much longer, but I'm grateful for the respite nonetheless."

The man led him into a small, crowded inn that was welcoming in its way. The air was thick with smoke and the smells of ale and of roots stewing in a meat broth; Niccolo's mouth watered. He'd grown up on the wine and finer fare of the south countries, but after more than a week of eating mostly dried fruit and hard meat and bread, anything hot and hearty smelled wonderful. His host caught sight of his face and said, "The stew I cannot offer you on the house, but if you've a coin or two, there's no reason you shouldn't feast as hearty as any man of the village and farms hereabouts."

"I might be able to manage that," Niccolo confessed, settling down on a wooden bench at a table. The man had been right about his condition. He hated to admit it, but he was worn through.

"You say you have not much farther to go," the innkeeper said, setting a tankard of ale before Niccolo. "Where be your destination?"

"The castle of Franz Bertoller," Niccolo answered.

"Indeed?" the innkeeper asked, his bushy eyebrows shooting up. "Strange business thereabouts, these days! But I don't know how a southerner such as you would have heard about it so quickly."

"I haven't heard," Niccolo said. "I am going there for reasons of my own. Can you tell me what's happening there?"

"Death was happening," the innkeeper said, "a mighty plague that swept much of the country, though it left us pretty much alone. But then yesterday some began to come through the town what said a miracle had come—that the nearly dead rose from their beds and walked upon seeing the face of a painting."

Niccolo shot to this feet in his excitement. He lowered himself again, aware that he'd spilled ale all over the table with his abrupt motion. The innkeeper didn't seem to care. "Did they say anything about a woman?" Niccolo asked.

"Aye, the painting was of a woman. A servant girl, they say. Mighty strange, the whole story."

"I don't think that would be the one. More likely they would say she was a noblewoman—for she carries herself like one, though she is a humble sister of the Oneness."

A darkness came over the man's face, and he looked about him as though afraid of eavesdroppers. "The Oneness, you say? That's a bad business in these parts, boy, a bad business indeed."

Niccolo frowned. "What can you mean?"

"The lord of the castle is no friend to the Oneness," the man said. "His father courted their favour, but the younger Bertoller had them all killed many years hence. His has been a foul lordship, but that deed was one of the foulest."

Alarm rose in Niccolo's heart as his mind raced back to his boyhood and the northern nobleman who had taken him from his parents on the road and brought him to the abbey and Teresa. He had never liked Franz Bertoller back then, but had always felt somewhat indebted to him, and he was too young to understand what Teresa really thought of him or why the sisters had asked the lord to withdraw his help and leave the abbey for good. He was sure that, whatever else might have been true, they had not viewed the man as an enemy—not a murderous one, in any case.

So they could not have known this part of his history.

"How many years hence did that happen?" Niccolo asked.

The innkeeper gave him a date, and Niccolo nodded—it had been some time before Franz Bertoller ever came to the abbey in the south countries. Apparently the lord had concealed much from the sisters.

"And the rumours you hear of the castle—they say nothing of a woman?"

"Not that I've heard, but those with stories to tell passed through quickly. They were sick, you see, and were healed, and all eager to get back home. As I said, the plague has largely left our folk be. Don't know the reason for that, but I'm grateful."

"You are under the Spirit's protection," Niccolo said. "May his grace rest on you."

"I don't know much about any of that," the man said. "I do know our kind never took up much with the lord. He's a crafty one, going in for intrigues and covenants and shadowy deals, and worse—the man deals with dark spirits, they say. Our folk are more honest than that. We pay taxes and let him alone, and he lets us alone in return."

His errand suddenly feeling that much more urgent, Niccolo rose to go. His host pushed him back down with a hand on his shoulder. "There now. Ye still need to eat something or you'll not get far. I don't like to remark upon it, but ye look as though there's a touch of the fever upon yourself. Will do you no good to starve your body besides."

Niccolo submitted, again forced to concede the man was right. His mind whirred over what he had just learned but could come up with no other plan than to leave as soon as possible, rush to Teresa's side, and rescue her from any threat. He had never been a man of craft, preferring to take the most direct course and stick passionately to it. It seemed to him that his benefactor was being obstinately slow about bringing his bowl of stew, but then, perhaps the man was trying to help him—make sure he actually took the rest he needed.

When the stew did come, Niccolo swallowed it too fast to taste it, scalding his tongue in the process.

"I thank you," he said, laying a small stack of coins on the table. "For the food, the drink, and your goodwill. And indeed for the tales you've told me."

"No trouble," the man replied. "I wish you well on your errand. Take care of yourself, lad; it's a cruel country you ride into."

Before he began to feel sick again, Niccolo had made good time. He anticipated that Franz Bertoller's city was only another day's ride, and as he urged his horse through the mountainous terrain thick with pines, he cast his spirit forward and tried to sense the presence of Oneness—of Teresa, not far away now. No assurance of connection came to him beyond what he and Teresa always shared—a heightened sense of the unity that bound all the Oneness together. That he had always, like a second breath in his lungs.

As a boy, some among the Oneness had been puzzled by Niccolo because it seemed that he had never Joined—the moment of entrance that every member of the Oneness treasured and forever remembered had never happened to him. This worried some, but wise Mother Isabel saw past it to the reality that Niccolo was already One. "Called from the womb," she had said. He did not know much about that. He only knew that Oneness was his whole life. Until the moment he met the sisters at the abbey, he had not understood who he was. But from that very moment, he had known himself to be forever home with them.

His failure to save them from the plague, so many years ago, still haunted him. He felt his gift for painting and creating wrestling in him, wanting out. But the very idea of loosing it brought back the crushing disappointment, the devastating helplessness of the day the plague was stronger and the sisters died.

The innkeeper's words spurred him on now. Franz Bertoller an enemy of the Oneness. And Teresa in his house. Miracles of healing happening, through a painting, as in the old days—but could the darkness see that as anything but a declaration of war?

She needed him.

He ignored waves of mild fever and pushed his horse onward, upward, into the mountains.

As the day wore on and the sun began to sink, he could feel the weariness in his steed but could not bear the thought of stopping for the night. Dark clouds were gathering overhead—storm clouds, he realized. He might want to push on through the night, but nature was unlikely to let him.

Unhappily accepting that to press on through a storm would likely get him lost, he began to look for shelter for the night. He found it in a shallow cave in a wall of black rock, reachable by an incline covered with shale. Pines clustered thickly around the slope, but the way itself was clear. He led his horse up the incline and freed it of its saddle, tethering it to a scraggly pine tree that was growing at the far end of the cave mouth.

It grew blacker by the moment, and by the time he had settled down in the back of the cave, rain started to fall. Within minutes the rain had grown to a deluge, and streams began to pour over the cave mouth, trapping him behind a variegated wall of water. His own corner remained reasonably dry, and he wrapped himself in his coat and resigned himself to spending the night out here.

He did not expect the demon attack and had no warning but for the sword that formed in his hand, fully there all at once. His body responded as though one with the weapon, leaping: he thrust it forward into the darkness even as claws and eyes and a great toothy maw appeared through the falling water and bore down on him. His sword thrust found purchase in the beast's shoulder—a bear, great and black, and animated by something far worse than any predator of the forest. It roared, Niccolo drove the sword harder, and he heard the shriek as demons rushed from the creature's body—but not before the terrible jaws had clamped onto his shoulder.

He heard his own shouts even as he did his best to twist the sword in deeper, and his knees buckled as pain seared through his body from his shoulder. He was pulled forward as the bear drew back and shook him, pulling him out into the rain. His body slammed against the rock wall and then his hands and face were being skinned against the shale and the bear had released its bite.

He heard demons shrieking through the darkness and his horse crying out in terror.

Then nothing more.

* * * * *

"I found him," Richard announced, standing as he shuffled files back into a neat stack. "It's a sixteen-hour drive. Who's coming?"

"I am," said nearly everyone. April's eyes filled with tears, and she uncurled herself slowly from the chair. "Thank you."

"He's our boy too," Richard said.

"Can we leave right away?"

"Far as I know."

"I need to go up to the cottage," April said. "Just to get something."

"Fine," Chris said. "My truck's there anyway, and we should take it. We're going to need a few cars."

April nodded dumbly, and not fifteen minutes later she was standing in the fishing cottage up on the cliff, rooting through her things for a sketchbook. She'd been drawing pictures for Nick, and she wanted to give them to him as soon as they found him.

She straightened when the phone rang.

Chris was outside starting the truck; she was the only one there.

It rang again.

And she knew—

She knew it was him.

"Hello?" she asked, her hands shaking.

"April?"

"Nick, thank God. Where are you?"

"I need you to come," Nick said. His voice trembled.

"We're coming, Nick. Where are you? Are you with your mom's boyfriend—Tom?"

"No, I ran away. I hate him. I hate it there."

"You ran away?" She forced her voice to stay calm. "Nick, where are you? We can't come get you if we don't know where you are."

"I'm not sure. I'm at the shipyards. In Bywater."

She closed her eyes. Bywater was only a few hours north of here—it was only by the Spirit's grace that he had called exactly now, before they all hit the road and went too far to be any help.

"Where's your mom?" April asked.

"I don't know. Probably with him. I thought I could hitch a ride home, but they were gonna call the cops on me so I ran."

Chris appeared in the kitchen doorway, a questioning look on his face. She waved for him to stay put and mouthed Nick's name.

"Okay, listen, Nick, do you see anywhere safe where you can wait? A restaurant or an office or something?"

"They'll call the cops on me."

"That's not a bad idea," April said. "You can wait at the police station."

His voice got stubborn. "I don't want to. Just come get me."

She thought better of arguing. Probably better for them all that they didn't involve the police again anyway. "Okay. Fine. But you need to wait somewhere safe."

"I'm safe. I'm where they build the ships. By the dock. There's a phone there. That's where I am."

She had to marvel at his nerve. But then, she knew too well what was driving it. She could still feel the sense of his distress, and its echoes in her own memories.

Memories that would always be a part of who she was, no matter how much she didn't want them to be.

Hanging up, she told Chris, "He's in Bywater. At the ship-yards. He ran away from Shelley and hitched a ride or something . . . don't ask me."

"That's good," Chris said. "He's not far; we can get him tonight."

"Yeah," April said. "But I'm not going to be happy until we've actually got him, so let's get going."

Chris nodded. "I'll call over and let everyone else know. You and me can just hit the road now. No reason to wait."

April appreciated that more than she could say. She had barely had time to buckle up in the truck before Chris joined her and they were on their way.

Nick sat huddled between a couple of oil drums on the dock near the shipyards, shivering in the orange light as snowflakes drifted lazily down. It was incredibly lonely to be engulfed by the night in such a world as this. But he liked that loneliness better than what he'd run from, because here was alone and waiting for the Oneness, his real family, to come and get him. And before he had been trapped with people he didn't trust, speeding up the highway toward a future he didn't want, inwardly alone and outwardly without any control at all.

Now, though, as he shivered in the cold and listened to the mingled sounds of machinery running and water washing up against the docks and people shouting somewhere at a distance, he had to wonder if he'd done something stupid by running away.

At least he'd reached April on the phone. She would be here soon. But it was cold.

And as much as he hated to admit it, he was scared.

There was some kind of menace in the air here that he had not expected. Like something . . .

He chilled through as he recognized the sensation.

Something demonic.

Something like what they had encountered when they were fighting the hive, and the evil was after them all the time.

But why would anything like that be here?

Because of you, he told himself. Because they want to kill you, Nick.

That makes no sense, he argued back. I'm just a kid.

He tried to rewind his memory, think over what had gotten him here. He'd run from his mother and Tom at a gas stop when they weren't looking. That wasn't hard—there had been slot machines inside, and they were inside playing. They left him for hours. So he just took off.

When you were scared, he told himself, accusingly.

That was true. He hadn't just decided to run. He'd felt, suddenly and forcefully, horribly afraid. So he had bolted, without much foresight and definitely without any real plan.

He'd run up the highway a ways, slowed down, and decided he was going home. He hated his mother. He hated Tom. He wanted to go back to the Oneness, and his mother and Tom had no right to take him away. He knew they weren't planning to bring him back—they didn't exactly try to hide anything from him. They talked in front of him like he was two years old and couldn't understand what they were saying.

So then he'd tried to hitch a ride, and one guy gave him a

ride a little ways, and then the next person said he was going to call the police, and when he stopped to use a payphone, Nick ran again.

Why had he done that?

The police might have helped him out. He knew there was dirt to find on Tom. They might have let him go home and protected him from his mother and her boyfriend. At first he'd been okay with the idea that the cops would come get him.

But then the fear again.

It had come hammering at him out of nowhere, so he couldn't even breathe. And he'd run once more.

He leaned against a stack of pallets and tried to sink deeper into his coat to keep warm. His duffel bag, stuffed with all the belongings he'd been able to bring with him, was wedged between him and one of the oil drums. He wanted it to warm up like a pillow, but it was just too cold outside.

What if the demons just came after him?

What if they possessed some stray dogs and came and tore him to pieces?

Fear was swelling up in his throat again, choking off his air supply. But this time he couldn't run. He couldn't move. He was sure if he peeked out over the oil drums, something with teeth and claws would be there and rip him to shreds.

And that wouldn't even be as bad as the fear—as feeling what it felt like to look into the eyes of something like that just before it killed you.

His heart pounding, he closed his eyes like he could shut out the fear and the threat that way. Like maybe if he couldn't see it, it couldn't see him.

Whatever "it" was.

Hurry, April. Hurry and come and find me.

A loud clanging of machinery not far away made the oil drums and the pallets and the ground under him tremble, like an earthquake. If something was sneaking up on him, he'd never even hear it.

Maybe it would be a bear.

He didn't know why that image came into his head.

Maybe the demon would come in the image of a huge, black bear, with enormous teeth and long claws and eyes that were red as blood. It would come snarling over the oil drums and rip his head off.

Any second now.

His entire body was quivering. He was going to attract it—it was going to know he was there because he was shaking so hard, it would hear him and smell his fear.

Stop it, he told himself. Calm down.

But he was going to die. You couldn't calm down when you were going to die.

You couldn't stop it.

You couldn't.

The quivering in all of his body culminated in a scream that he couldn't keep down, and he leaped to his feet and ran.

* * * * *

Rachel Starr Thomson

Niccolo dreamed.

He saw a boy a world away. One like himself in many ways—full of fire, full of art, full of the Spirit and of life. And threatened.

He tried to speak to the boy, but could not.

The boy thought he was alone. Alone in a dark world full of water, machinery, and enormous ships. But Niccolo could see what the boy could not: that the air all around him was filled with others. Demons prowled the perimeter of an angelic guard. Some of the cloud stood and watched, whispering things to the child that he could not hear.

Niccolo thought a great battle was about to break out between the Oneness and the demons. A battle for this boy: for his life and his heart.

Of all the demons, the worst had the form of a gigantic black bear with teeth and claws like spearhooks. Niccolo could feel the force of those teeth, clamped into his shoulder, dragging him, shaking him—

He woke up gasping in the rain.

His body was burning with fever and weak from loss of blood. Pain still seared through him from his shoulder, and turning his head slightly, he could make out a dark blotch that covered as much as he could see of that side of his body. Though the sky was still darkened by clouds and rain, the sun must have risen, for he could see too well for it to be night.

Shivering and shaking, he forced himself to roll over and then curled up into a ball, unable to go any further. He could hear the voice of his horse not far away, as though the beast was encouraging him to uncurl himself and keep coming back to shelter. But he could not. The pain and the illness were too great.

He turned his head slightly, and his eyes fell on a hulking black shape. The bear. Dead. He knew he had not mortally wounded it; the demons themselves must have killed it as they tore out of its body at the insistence of Niccolo's sword.

His had never been a life of warfare. Only a few times had he ever faced such creatures, and always on behalf of someone else. Why they had come here, into this forsaken and desolate place, he could not imagine.

Unless they had not been here by chance.

They might have been sent to kill him.

The answer came to him all at once.

To stop him from reaching Teresa.

He forced himself to uncurl. Forced his quivering arm to stretch out and his legs to pull up beneath him; forced himself to his feet. He leaned on the rock wall as he hobbled toward the cave entrance and all but fell inside.

It was still dry where he had sheltered until the attack in the night. But he was soaked, and he could not escape himself or his clothing. He cast a helpless look at his horse, which looked back and shook its head. Forcing himself onto his feet again, he lurched forward, using his good arm to balance himself against the back of the cave, until he reached his horse and let himself fall against it. Its body was warm and dry, and he stood there, leaning his whole weight into the animal, good hand tangled in its mane, soaking up the warmth.

He had to reach Teresa. Somehow, he had to overcome this and get to her. If he had doubted the urgency of his errand, if he'd thought himself spurred on only by his own desire to see her and be near her, he had no doubts now. The need was dire.

Indeed, he had no doubt the need was mortal.

My good innkeeper, he thought in the direction of the village, I would call you to my aid now. I could use more than a rest and a drink, I fear.

But of course, there was no aid here.

He sank to his knees, unable to stand any longer, and shivered against the rock. His whole shoulder was throbbing, and from the warmth he could now feel trickling its way across his shoulder and chest, he judged that the bleeding had resumed.

Teresa, he cast out. Teresa, if you can hear me, I am coming to you—but I am in need of your help now.

He closed his eyes and concentrated on breathing. It seemed his lungs wanted to stop, but he could not allow them to play that trick on him.

Pray. He could pray, should pray. Reach out not merely to the Oneness but directly to the Spirit who inspired them.

That Spirit who was his earliest and oldest companion.

"Help me," he prayed. "Speed me on my way."

From deep within words began to form on his tongue, words placed there by another though it was his voice that gave them utterance. He could not understand them, but he felt the deep strength and comfort they imparted.

A reminder that even as he prayed in the depths of a feverish wilderness, he was not alone, and his prayers were not alone nor of his own making.

But his body went cold—very cold—as the last of the prayers trembled through his lips, and he knew the breath that followed them would be his last. Death had stopped him.

His lungs curled in on themselves and went hard, and he rolled up tightly on the ground and died.

And then Breath swept through him—he could hear it, rushing in his ears, the breath of the universe, the life of God. It rushed through his body and animated his lungs again, and he was breathing, gasping, and full of light—the whole sky, the mountains, the world above him, pulsating with light.

His eyes were open, his back to the ground, and he blinked up at the sky.

Alive.

And the shape of a man was fading away from before him. As though just a moment ago the man had been clear to his eyes, and they had sat and talked as friends, but now he was leaving, and Niccolo could not quite remember his face or what they had said . . .

Alive.

And stronger. He moved his fingers and then his arm at the elbow, and everything worked as it should. He could still feel blood and water stiffening his clothing as they dried. Sometime between death and living again, the rain had stopped. But despite the blood, he could not feel a wound, and he felt—yes, he was, he tested it—he was strong enough to stand and ride and finish his journey after all.

It was a strange thing, to have faced the end of everything and then discovered it was not the end at all.

A smile quirked his lips as he understood something for the first time: that even had the breath not come sweeping back through him, even if the Spirit had not reanimated his body and given him back his days on earth, he would have discovered that death was not the end.

Not at all.

"But a terrible thing nonetheless," he muttered. And it was true. Having tasted death, he felt within him a deep distaste for it. It was the opposite of Spirit and life and Oneness; it was corruption and a deep and terrible fracture in the unity that was meant to be.

He understood for the first time that Death was the enemy and that Oneness would overcome it. That they had to overcome it. It was why they existed.

Or else it was the only thing preventing them from truly knowing why they existed, and only when it was gone would they discover that at last.

* * * * *

The sensation of Nick's renewed distress slammed into April like a wrecking ball, and she gasped and lurched forward, grabbing the dashboard to steady herself. Chris swerved in response but quickly got the truck back under control, eyeing her as closely as he could without losing all attention on the road.

"Are you okay?" he asked.

"It's Nick. Something's really wrong. He's terrified."

"You think it's demons?"

She closed her eyes.

Yes, she did.

She remembered the terrors she'd felt at various times in the battle with the hive—the first time she was abducted, and the encounter with the man sent to kill her in the cell house, and the creature that hunted her along the coastal shore. Nick felt that terror. A kind of fear that stemmed from something more primal and horrible than the filtered evil of human beings.

"Yeah," she said. "Can you go faster?"

"Going as fast as I can." But he sped up anyway. "I don't get this!" he said. "We beat them, didn't we? How are they coming after us again?"

"We beat the people," April said. She hadn't even realized the truth until she said it, now, speeding up the coast toward Bywater in the desperate hope of reaching Nick in time. They had beat the human leaders and thereby fractured the hive's power, but there were still spirits—demons—that could think and feel and that wanted revenge.

"Don't they need people? Demons don't just act by themselves, right?"

"They're using Shelley," April said.

"Shelley's not even there."

"But she's supposed to be caring for Nick—sheltering him, not exposing him. And his dad. His dad should be out there covering for him, not getting drunk in a pub while he lets us look for his son and indulges in bitter feelings toward his ex and her boyfriend."

April acknowledged the bitterness in her own tone, her own soul, as she spoke words she knew were true though she hadn't formulated them till now.

Parents were supposed to cover their children.

And when they didn't, it tore a hole open over kids like Nick, and like April herself, that made them vulnerable in a way they were never meant to be.

Which meant Nick wasn't just afraid for no reason. The danger he was in was real.

It all came crashing together. Shelley and her husband and their irresponsibility and selfishness had left Nick exactly where the demonic wanted him:

Where they could get to him and hurt the Oneness.

Where they could tear into the village cell with all the ferocity of grief and loss and heartache.

Maybe after all, it wasn't just Oneness who were inextricably linked to one another. Maybe the whole human race was linked, so tightly that no one could act without in some way affecting everyone else.

Her head spun.

A highway sign announced Bywater in fifteen miles.

Fifteen miles that might mean forever.

* * * * *

Nick's heart was pounding so hard that he couldn't see

straight; the whole dimly lit, fiery world in front of him was a wash, a blur of nightmarish machinery and orange light.

He knew something was there. The bear he'd imagined. Just beyond his eyesight. He'd run in one direction as hard as he could, skidding and falling and scrambling back to his feet to run again, and then scathing fear warned him to turn around, so he did. And ran and skidded and scrambled until fear told him to turn again, and he ran another way, and every way he went, he hit invisible walls of fear.

So finally he found a little spot in the midst of a tangle of machinery he couldn't identify. He slipped into cracks and between tightly packed vehicles and cranes until he reached a spot the size of a barrel in the midst of it all, and he curled himself up there and cried like a baby.

Why wasn't anyone here to save him?

Why was his dad still so far away?

Why didn't his mother care about him?

Why were even the Oneness not here yet? He knew April was coming . . . she had promised. And April never broke her promises.

He remembered fish and chips at the pub, and a new sketchbook, and the drawings he was supposed to be working on for her.

He wished she would come fast so all those things would really happen.

His face was a mass of tears and mucous and his sides and his eyes hurt from crying, but he couldn't make himself stop.

Even though he was sure the sound was alerting them all

to where he was.

The demons were coming.

He could see them now—in the shadows.

The shadows were growing and taking form and looming over the tops of the machines.

In his hand, he felt something hard.

He looked down and saw, forming before his eyes, a sword.

It was small. Like a toy. Nothing compared to the swords he'd seen some of the others carrying—Reese and Tyler and Richard. Theirs were great weapons in great hands.

This was just a dagger clutched in the fist of a little boy.

But as he stared at it, his tears began to dry and his vision to clear.

Before he ran from his mother and Tom, he'd been drawing a comic book about Richard. He was really proud of a panel that showed a battle, with enormous demons and a sword in Richard's hand that Nick had patterned after one he'd seen in the movies. And Richard had another weapon: his words. His voice that could stop the enemy in their tracks. He had drawn Richard shouting words that sent the enemy spinning away in a panic.

He'd wanted to be like that someday.

He'd dreamed of doing great things with a sword and a voice and his drawings, like April's.

"Okay," he whispered. "Okay, Nick. If you've only got one shot, then make it a good one."

He cleared his throat and tightened his grip on the little sword, still staring hard at it.

He felt . . . alone.

And not alone.

He straightened his legs and stood in the little barrel-shaped hole, and he stared up at the shadows and the things he was sure were lurking there.

Doing his best to imitate Richard's deep tones, he shouted, "You are not going to win!"

The shout came out as more of a squeak, but he cleared his throat and tried again.

"The Spirit is greater than you are! And the Oneness is more powerful! You see this sword in my hand?"

He waved the dagger in the air, feeling braver as he did, even though his voice wanted to crack again. He forced it to hold steady. "I am going to take you down with me!"

Above him, directly in front of him, something enormous was starting to form in the shadows just above and beyond a crane truck. Something with huge shoulders and a huge head and huge teeth . . .

Nick turned and darted through a crack in the machinery and started to run for open spaces.

He hadn't planned to do that, but instinct kicked in and told him he wasn't going to win a fight if he didn't even have room to move.

Behind him, something roared.

Its voice was so strong it rattled the machinery and made the ground shake.

Julie still didn't understand why she was alive. The question plagued her at times.

Alex was sitting in their living room watching TV, and Miranda was popping in and out of the kitchen and her bedroom, staying mostly away from Alex but getting close enough to say hello or get a look at him every time she walked into the kitchen. Julie had stopped counting the reasons she found to go in there: need a cup of tea, need to wash the cup, need to find a pencil, need to look something up. Andrew had decided it was best if Alex and Miranda didn't actually interact, so he'd banished their daughter to her bedroom.

It felt good to have someone else laying down the law. Especially Andrew. Even with all his distrust of her, she trusted his heart.

She was also glad that whatever was alive in Alex, it seemed content to remain dormant for now. The TV watching was annoying—she'd lived without any media intrusion for fifteen years, and she found television especially to be incredibly intrusive and grating—but it was better than a demonic manifestation anyday, especially considering that the demon or demons inside the teen quite likely wanted her dead.

Which brought her back to the question of why she was alive.

Had any other member of the Oneness, in all of history, ever been raised from the dead?

She filed that away to ask Richard. He might know. She had asked the Spirit, but he hadn't answered. She had quickly learned that the Spirit who presumably knew all things was not prone to giving answers to everything all the time, though she did have a strong sense that he liked for her to search for them.

Maybe you value something more if you have to search for it, she thought.

Maybe that was why not all answers came easily.

Deep in thought as she was, it took a moment before she realized the TV had been turned off.

Miranda had gone back upstairs; the house was silent except for the ticking of the clock on the kitchen wall.

"Andrew?" she turned slowly, dreading to see what might be standing behind her in the door between the kitchen and the living room.

Alex was there.

And his eyes had disappeared in a wash of darkness.

* * * * *

Nick's mad scramble through the machines brought him out into the open again, into the glare of orange lights where the sounds of distant workers could reach him. For a second he wondered if he should keep running and try to reach them—if the men at work building ships could help protect him.

But his feet didn't want to move anymore.

Even though his legs were shaking and his whole face was twitching with nervous energy, he had to stand.

Face the enemy.

Not lead the demons to other people who they could hurt or possess.

He was Oneness. It was his job to protect.

Even if nobody was there to protect him.

It was his job to fight the enemy.

So that was what he was going to do.

He spread his feet out in a fighting stance and held his dagger at the ready. "Come on!" he called. "Let's see you!"

Whether his words actually called the demons into visible form or whether they would have materialized anyway, he didn't know. But suddenly, there they were. The bear—huge, black, clawed and toothed and red-eyed, and about to rip his head off, just like he'd imagined it.

And a lot of others, too.

And beyond them—

Others.

His breath caught, because he wasn't alone. Not at all.

Rise   269

Wreathing the entire arena was a cloud—silver and misty and made up of figures, figures even the demons could not see.

Some were men and women. Three stood together, a man with dark hair and two women, one a redhead and one beautiful and foreign-looking. Some were creatures with wings and animal heads and many eyes. Some looked like people, even children, but they were not—something about their eyes was different. Watchers, he thought. Like Chris had told him about.

They were all watching him, and they all had encouragement and joy in their faces.

The bear advanced and reared up on its hind legs. Nick crouched and prepared to drive his dagger into its heart. He yelled.

The entire cloud yelled along with him.

A battle cry.

And a wave of heat blew through the industrial complex and sent machines and pallets and demons flying.

* * * * *

"Alex," Julie said. "Alex. Come back. You're in there . . . come back."

A sword was forming itself in her hand. She knew, from Reese, that this was what happened when Oneness and the demonic came into each other's active presence. Instant defense.

But she closed her hand and wished it away.

It vanished.

She stood empty-handed.

Andrew was somewhere—in the garage, maybe. Working on his truck. Or trying to talk to Miranda.

She could scream for him and he would come, but not fast enough. Wherever he was, he wouldn't get here soon enough to make the difference needed.

The boy's eyes were staring into hers, but they weren't eyes—there were no whites, no pupils, no colour. They were black holes. Windows into an abyss far deeper than one young man's soul.

Into death itself.

This was not just a demon.

"Alex," she said again, her voice calmer than she could understand. She didn't understand what possessed her at this moment, why she was not terrified, why she did not want to fight.

Except that fighting this would kill the boy, and she didn't want that.

She didn't want to give death any victory at all.

Still he did not answer, or move. He stood in the doorway in the silence and stared.

The eyes were beckoning her.

Trying to suck her in.

Trying to pull her back.

"No," she said, and now she was not speaking to the boy any longer. "You did not win. Even if I had died, you would have not won—you would not have held me. The light would still have rescued me."

His hand shot out and touched her shoulder.

Cold pierced through her to the heart. She gasped and struggled to keep standing; she was on her knees—did not know when she had fallen—and then she did not think she was in her body any more at all.

She stood on a vast, empty plain.

Darkness everywhere. Not the starry, moonlit darkness of night, but a deeper black, an emptiness, a void.

A being with no face stood before her, still dressed in her husband's clothes, still wearing the frame of a teenage boy.

And yet nameless, faceless.

A nothing.

No soul, no true being at all. A negation of being.

She was colder than she knew it was possible to be, yet she did not shiver.

The creature in front of her stood utterly still.

It did not, she realized, even breathe.

It could not. This place was without air, without atmosphere.

So how was it that she was breathing?

For she most certainly was.

And with every breath, the deadness and void of this place quaked.

She felt that deep within its core—it shook as though in fear.

It was not air she breathed in and then let out again.

Rather, she was breathing from something within herself and then releasing it into the void.

And as she did, the void itself began to change.

It began with light.

Far off, on the horizon, pulsing to the rhythm of her lungs. And then rising as a sun.

Its rays burst out over the land, piercing through the silent figure of Death before her.

She raised her hands high and heard herself cry out words that, like the breath in her lungs, came from somewhere deep inside herself and transformed the landscape around her:

"Let there be life!"

She blinked, and she was in the kitchen. Back on her feet, somehow. And the boy, Alex, was crumpled prostrate at her feet.

The TV was still on.

"Julie?" Andrew's voice said, sharply, from behind her.

But the news anchor's voice had already arrested her attention.

"A massive fire has broken out in a shipyard in Bywater. Authorities say all workers are accounted for, but there may be someone else still trapped in the blaze . . ."

* * * * *

Not one of us knows who we are.

It's clearer when you've crossed into the cloud . . . but even then, much is shrouded in mystery.

Not one of us knows.

Not one of us . . .

April stood in the midst of the shipyard and burned.

The flames licked up masts and scaffolding and warehouse walls, oil drums and pallets and netting and machinery. The sky and water themselves were ablaze, and April in the centre of it all stood and regarded it and saw.

She saw that though all was on fire, nothing here burned.

Nothing here would burn.

Nothing except those things that were invisible to everyone but her—

For this was a purifying fire.

The human side of the hive had perished in the first fire, in the cemetery. Bertoller forever finished, Jacob gone, David saved—though to what end remained to be seen.

But the demonic side had not. The core, fed so long by so much evil, had retained much power, and they had concentrated here and gone after Nick.

She should have seen it coming.

They all should have known the enemy had not given up.

She of all people should have known that where the Spirit rose up in strength, manifesting himself in power, everything in creation that was not of the Spirit would betray itself in protest.

But Teresa's words still repeated in her memory.

Not one of us knows who we are.

Or what we are, April thought.

Or what dwells within us.

Not one of us knows what it is, who it is, that seeks One-ness with us.

Nick cowered behind her, clutching her leg, afraid but riveted.

By the glory of the flames.

And April, this time, only smiled and waited and watched as the fire burned and the enemy alone, the enemy out of every-thing here, the enemy whose forms and voices she could only just make out in the pure flame, was consumed.

The fire had been there after all. Not for her to conjure up or manipulate, but there, hot, ready to burn for its own purposes as soon as she agreed to those purposes. The enemy had gath-ered together—all of them, every spirit that had battled them in the hive, every regional terror that haunted the coast. Drawn by one small boy's vulnerability, and by a hatred and desire for revenge that made them blind to the way they courted their own destruction.

That was how, in the end, the darkness would fall. Through its own mad desire to destroy at all costs, a desire that would cheat and betray them in the end.

On the perimeter of the shipyards she could see and hear fire trucks and news vans; a helicopter passed overhead for the second time. If anyone could see them, she had no idea. The fire did not smoke, but it was so bright as to be nearly impossible to look into. Chris was back there somewhere, maybe trying to explain.

Or maybe he was just trying to keep out of sight or pretend to be an innocent bystander, because who could explain this?

Who would believe it?

Who except those who, through experience and asking, had grown ears to hear?

You couldn't tell news reporters that the shipyards were on fire with the very Spirit that sustained all life and gave them the very breath in their lungs, and that the flames raged because they were consuming the demonic, the darkness, the enemy; and that what would be left when the fire died out would be a new beginning for the entire coast. That somehow the warfare one little group of people in a fishing village had been waging, a warfare of love and of connection and of sacrifice and of service, had culminated here and that this was victory.

And what would she tell them, if they asked her questions? Could she tell them that the fire was burning out of her the old fears, the old distrusts, even the sting of the old memories—that it was purifying her soul and making something new of her life, something that did not negate the old but transformed it?

What would Nick tell them, if he were asked?

So she smiled.

Smiled and waited and let the brightness drop another layer of scales from her eyes.

* * * * *

Reese slammed the car door and ran to Chris's side. The others were behind her—spilling out of the two vehicles they had brought after Chris and April sped out ahead of them.

"Wow," she said as she stepped up beside Chris and let him close her hand in his.

"Yeah," he answered.

"This is it, isn't it?" Reese asked. "The end of the war."

"The end of the battle, anyway," Chris said.

They watched the fire raging. Not a hundred feet away, fire-trucks were pouring water into it, but they made little difference. News vans and the first crowds of onlookers were gathering, providing effective camouflage for the Oneness cell.

"When does the war end?" Reese asked after a while.

"When we defeat death," Melissa answered. Reese looked over at her, and Melissa smiled.

"When we all become One," Tyler put in.

"When no one is outside of love anymore," Richard finished. "Or outside of life."

"When fear is conquered," Diane said.

"When forgiveness is the crown jewel," Mary said with a smile.

They fell silent again for a long time, watching the beauty and ferocity of the flame. They all knew what was happening— they could feel it, almost see it. The purifying of the air. The ridding the world of spirits that were against them.

"They're okay, right?" Chris asked.

Richard smiled. "Of course they are."

The village surrounding the castle on a hill was eerily silent and still as Niccolo rode in at the end of a thunderous ride, only a day after his death and resurrection in the depths of the forest. Could he have carried himself on his own two feet, he thought his heart might have pushed him so hard he could have made it sooner—but as it was, his horse could do no more than the momentous effort it did put forth.

Chimneys, and the hearths beneath them, were cold. No one stirred in the streets, no movement rustled behind windows. To all appearances, the place was abandoned.

Above the valley, the castle loomed ominous on the hilltop.

"Whoa, boy." He patted his horse's neck and dismounted, looking around for any sign of life. Nothing. A watering trough stood full, and he led his horse to it and let the animal drink while he gazed pensively up at the castle.

He had thought to ride directly to Teresa's rescue. But he was faced, now, with the necessity of finding her first.

What if the castle was as abandoned as this village appeared to be?

He sent his heart out ahead of him, reaching up to the castle—

And found someone.

Oneness.

A faint life, in trouble, but living still.

He made to remount his horse and thought better of it. The animal had come too far, worked too hard; he couldn't push it any further now. "I'll be back for you," he told it, and then he tore up the village street straight for the castle gates.

They hung open. No guard stood duty. The courtyard on the other side was an eerie ghost town: full of tents and pallets—a hospital, he realized. Teresa's work, surely. But there were no patients, nor any dead. It seemed everyone had been spirited away.

But no.

Someone was here.

Teresa, he told himself. It was Teresa. He could feel the bond of Oneness tugging at him. It had to be her.

Closing his eyes a moment, he let the sensation pull him across the courtyard, where he stumbled on something—

A thin panel of wood.

Heart pounding, he flipped it over to find a painting, unmistakably Teresa's work, though it had been slashed and defaced. Still, he could make out the luminous features of a young woman with wiry red hair and high cheekbones, an image that stirred him even in its corrupted form. The face was life.

The Oneness tugged harder at him, and he dropped the painting and stumbled forward. The pull was taking on words in his heart and mind:

Help me.

Quickly.

I need you.

His feet were pounding the flagstones before he was even aware that they knew where to go; then his eyes recognized a chapel just beyond the castle, and he was running, racing to get there before it was too late.

He burst through the door.

And his heart dropped.

A young woman lay on the floor at the foot of the altar, a pool of blood forming around her. Yet he could see her breathing—she was alive. Her face was turned away from him, but he recognized the red hair and knew the features would be those in the painting.

But she was not Teresa.

And he could not feel Teresa anywhere.

He hesitated in the chapel door.

It was not often in life that a man could see exactly that he stood at a crossroads, and that one choice would take away the other, never to be recovered.

He knew it now.

That if he stayed here, if he helped this girl, he would never find Teresa.

That if he rushed away, followed his heart, answered the urgency pounding in his ears, he might yet be able to help the woman who had been to him more than a sister, more than a mother, who had been one with him in a way only great spirits could be one.

But this girl, this stranger who was yet Oneness, would die.

She stirred.

Tearless, stronger than he'd known he could be, he passed through the door and knelt beside her. Gently lifting her head and shoulders, he gazed on the face that Teresa had painted—the life she had recognized as something beautiful.

"It's all right," he told the girl. "I will help you. You will live."

"He has taken her," the girl choked. "The lord has taken her away . . ."

"I know," Niccolo whispered.

His heart stretched out to someplace unknown and said good-bye.

He hoped that she heard him.

In a cave deep in the rock of the mountains, trapped behind a wall of stone so thick and impenetrable that no man would ever be able to move it again, Teresa closed her eyes and smiled.

Good-bye, Niccolo, she answered him back. Follow me to the end. Paint again. Be the great one I saw in my vision so long ago. There is life in you, and it will be greater than death. I promise you that.

His thoughts, his pain, came to her from far away.

But why must it be this way? May I not even see you again?

Not now, she answered him. One day. I will see you in the cloud. And again, in the flesh. We will all be whole again, Niccolo.

She had already begun to starve.

But she was not afraid.

She told him so, and sent one final thought to him:

Do not fear, my friend. Nothing ends here. We may fall, but know this:

We will rise.

* * * * *

Bundled in blankets, Nick slept in the backseat of Chris's truck. Reese and April had crammed into the front seat next to Chris, and April kept her eyes on the child as they drove home.

"You should have seen him," she said. "Standing there like he was going to take down the whole demon army by himself. He didn't even look scared."

"Maybe he couldn't see them," Chris said.

"He saw them."

"Maybe he could see something else," Reese remarked.

April turned around and settled back into her seat and closed her eyes.

Thank you, she prayed.

You're welcome, the still voice in her soul answered.

Not just for saving him, she continued.

What else?

She struggled to put words to it.

For . . . for answering me. For proving that I can trust you.

A long time passed as the truck made its way home toward the fishing village. Reese and Chris talked in low tones; April found it easy to shut their conversation out.

The conversation within her began again with the Spirit asking a question.

If things had turned out differently, would that have proven that I am not trustworthy?

She thought it over. No. I don't know.

You will know, one day. You will know me.

She smiled. I want that.

And the Spirit answered: Bit by bit, as you are ready, you will all know me. And we will defeat the darkness.

Forever.

Rachel Starr Thomson

Rachel would love to hear from you!

You can visit her and interact online:
Web: **www.rachelstarrthomson.com**
Facebook: **www.facebook.com/RachelStarrThomsonWriter**
Twitter: **@writerstarr**

THE SEVENTH WORLD TRILOGY

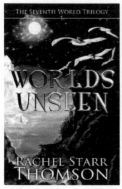  

Worlds Unseen   Burning Light   Coming Day

For five hundred years the Seventh World has been ruled by a tyrannical empire—and the mysterious Order of the Spider that hides in its shadow. History and truth are deliberately buried, the beauty and treachery of the past remembered only by wandering Gypsies, persecuted scholars, and a few unusual seekers. But the past matters, as Maggie Sheffield soon finds out. It matters because its forces will soon return and claim lordship over her world, for good or evil.

The Seventh World Trilogy is an epic fantasy, beautiful, terrifying, pointing to the realities just beyond the world we see.

"An excellent read, solidly recommended for fantasy readers."
– Midwest Book Review

"A wonderfully realistic fantasy world. Recommended."
– Jill Williamson, Christy-Award-Winning Author
of *By Darkness Hid*

"Epic, beautiful, well-written fantasy that sings of Christian truth."
– Rael, reader

Available everywhere online or special order from your local bookstore.

THE PROPHET TRILOGY

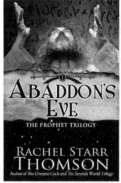  

Abaddon's Eve   Comes the Dragon   Beloved

A prophet and his apprentice.
A runaway and a wealthy widow marked as an outcast.

They alone can see the terrible judgment
marching on their land.

But can they do anything to stop it?

The Prophet Trilogy is a fantasy set in
a near-historical world of deserts, temples,
and spiritual forces that vie
for the hearts of men.

Available everywhere online or special order from your local bookstore.

TAERITH

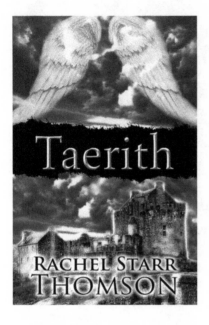

When he rescues a young woman named Lilia from bandits, Taerith Romany is caught in a web of loyalties: Lilia is the future queen of a spoiled king, and though Taerith is not allowed to love her, neither he can bring himself to leave her without a friend. Their lives soon intertwine with the fiercely proud slave girl, Mirian, whose tragic past and wild beauty make her the target of the king's unscrupulous brother.

The king's rule is only a knife's edge from slipping—and when it does, all three will be put to the ultimate test. In a land of fog and fens, unicorns and wild men, Taerith stands at the crossroads of good and evil, where men are vanquished by their own obsessions or saved by faith in higher things.

"Devastatingly beautiful . . . I am amazed at every chapter how deeply you've caused us to care for these characters."
—Gabi

"Deeply satisfying." —Kapezia

"Rachel Starr Thomson is an artist, and every chapter of Taerith is like a painting . . . beautiful."
—Brittany Simmons

Available everywhere online or special order from your local bookstore.

ANGEL IN THE WOODS

Hawk is a would-be hero in search of a giant to kill or a maiden to save. The trouble is, when he finds them, there are forty-some maidens— and they call their giant "the Angel." Before he knows what's happening, Hawk is swept into the heart of a patchwork family and all of its mysteries, carried away by their camaraderie— and falling quickly in love.

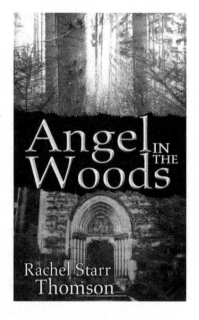

But the outside world cannot be kept at bay forever. Suspecting the Giant of hiding a treasure, the wealthy and influential Widow Brawnlyn sets out to tear the family apart and bring the Giant to destruction any way she can. And her two principle weapons are Hawk—and the truth.

Caught between the terrible truths he discovers about the family's past and the unalterable fact that he has come to love them, Hawk must face his fears and overcome his flaws if he is to rescue the Angel in the woods.

> *"A beautiful tale of finding oneself, honor and heroism; a story I will not soon forget."* — Szoch

> *"The more I think about it, the more truth and beauty I find in the story."* —H. A. Titus

Available everywhere online or special order from your local bookstore.

REAP THE WHIRLWIND

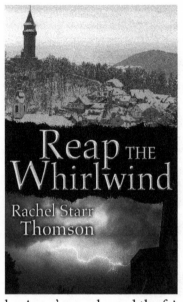

Beren is a city in constant unrest: ruled by a ruthless upper class and harried by a band of rebels who want change. Its one certainty is that the two sides do not, and will not, meet.

But children know little of sides or politics, and Anna and Kyara—a princess and a peasant girl—let their chance meeting grow into a deep friendship. Until the day Kyara's family is slaughtered by Anna's people, and the friendship comes to an abrupt end.

Years later, Kyara is a rebel—bitter, hard, and violent. Anna's efforts to fight the political system she belongs to avail little. Neither is a child anymore—but neither has ever forgotten the power of their long-ago friendship. When a secret plot brings the rebellion to a fiery head, both young women know it is too late to save the land they love.

But is it too late to save each other?

Available everywhere online.

LADY MOON

When Celine meets Tomas, they are in a cavern on the moon where she has been languishing for thirty days after being banished by her evil uncle for throwing a scrub brush at his head. Tomas is a charming and eccentric Immortal, hanging out on the moon because he's procrastinating his destiny—meeting, and defeating, Celine's uncle.

A pair of magic rings send them back to earth, where Celine insists on returning home and is promptly thrown into the dungeon. Her uncle, Ignus Umbria, is up to no good, and his latest caper threatens to devour the whole countryside. He doesn't want Celine getting in the way. More than that, he wants to force Tomas into a confrontation—and Tomas, who has fallen in love with Celine, cannot procrastinate any longer.

Lady Moon is a fast-paced, humorous adventure in a world populated by mad magicians, walking rosebushes, thieving scullery maids, and other improbable things. And of course, the most improbable—and magical—thing of all: true love.

"Celine's sarcastic 'languishing' immediately put me in mind of Patricia C. Wrede's Dealing with Dragons series—a fairy tale that gently makes fun of the usual fairy tale tropes. And once again, Rachel Starr Thomson doesn't disappoint."

— H. A. Titus

"Funny and quirky fantasy."

Available everywhere online.

THE ONENESS CYCLE

| Exile | Hive | Attack | Renegade | Rise |

*The supernatural entity called the Oneness holds the world together.
What happens if it falls apart?*

In a world where the Oneness exists, nothing looks the same.
Dead men walk. Demons prowl the air. Old friends peel back
their mundane masks and prove as supernatural as angels. But
after centuries of battling demons and the corrupting powers
of the world, the Oneness is under a new threat—its greatest
threat. Because this time, the threat comes from within.

Fast-paced contemporary fantasy.

*"Plot twists and lots of edge-of-your-seat action,
I had a hard time putting it down!"*
—Alexis

"Finally! The kind of fiction I've been waiting for my whole life!"
—Mercy Hope, FaithTalks.com

*"I sped through this short, fast-paced novel, pleased by the well-
drawn characters and the surprising plot. Thomson has done a
great job of portraying difficult emotional journeys . . . Read it!"*
—Phyllis Wheeler, The Christian Fantasy Review

Available everywhere online or special order from your local bookstore.

Short Fiction by Rachel Starr Thomson

BUTTERFLIES DANCING

FALLEN STAR

OF MEN AND BONES

OGRES IS

JOURNEY

MAGDALENE

THE CITY CAME CREEPING

WAYFARER'S DREAM

WAR WITH THE MUSE

SHIELDS OF THE EARTH

And more!

*Available as downloads for
Kindle, Kobo, Nook, iPad, and more!*

CPSIA information can be obtained
at www.ICGtesting.com
Printed in the USA
LVHW04s2330160818
587183LV00003B/223/P

9 781927 658338